Richard J. Beres

Seademons

Seademons

WITHDRAWN

A NOVEL BY

Laurence Yep

*To Richard,
One of the
good people
with fondest
wishes*

PERENNIAL LIBRARY
Harper & Row, Publishers
New York, Hagerstown, San Francisco, London

*Larry Yep
7/16/79*

To Leslie Fiedler and the Lanes—
John, Linda, Liz, and Jenny—
who never said,
"How outrageous."

First PERENNIAL LIBRARY edition published 1979.

ISBN: 0-06-080477-7

79 80 81 82 83 10 9 8 7 6 5 4 3 2 1

Seademons

one

They came with the rising of the moons when the sea was black and the night just begun. The Anglic with his keen old eyes saw them first; and when we looked between the everblues to where he pointed, we saw them too: the ripples, silvery in the moonlight, moving counter to the wind across the black water.

"Now remember," my stepbrother Athvel, whispered. "None of you are to shoot unless I give the word. We're here simply to see who our guests might be."

When we had first come to Fancyfree, twelve years ago, we had thought it free of intelligent life. The highest form of life had been the Seademons, which were large, squid-like animals that could communicate among themselves at what we thought was a primitive, animal level. But then last night we had met a farmer trekking over the hills from his holding because his radio had broken down—as was happening with so much of the precious equipment we had stolen from the Fair Folk. He had been on his way to the next holding to see if their radio worked, for just that morning he had found nearly half a hectare of wheat trampled flat and a robot deactivated by some intelligent hand.

I tensed as the ripples neared the shore, and I picked up my automatic crossbow. The sea surged up the beach and splashing through the surf came our six guests.

1

They were not Seademons. They were like nothing I had ever imagined.

"Are those the Fair Folk?" Athvel asked in a low, shocked voice.

The Anglic knew the question was meant for him. Of us all, he was the only one who had actually seen the Fair Folk. "No," he reassured us in a whisper, "those things aren't the Fair Folk, though they might be their troops. The people and worlds in their empire were beyond a person's counting."

But it was hard for me to believe that the Fair Folk of our tales could ever bring themselves to take the sword oaths of such monstrous creatures. They seemed the epitome of slimy, nightmarish slugs, leaving a shining trail behind them as they rolled up the sand.

In the moonlight the monsters' wet skins glistened an iridescent green shot with blue and purple patches through their coating of sand. At each end of their cylinder-shaped bodies they had a set of tentacles which could be retracted into hard red knobs. The large tentacles helped to push and pull their heavy bodies along while the smaller tentacles sniffed the air and the ground.

Despite myself, I found my hand touching Earthstuff. All the Folk had some charm associated with our lost home world, Tara. The usual kind of Earthstuff among the Folk was a common object that had been touched to the holy relics in the rectory. But I had a small amber bead in which a tiny Taran flower had been preserved and which had once belonged to my own mother and her mother before her in an unending line back to the ancient days of Tara. And for extra safety I made the sign of Sane Collen, sweeping the charm in my hand before me in the outline of a shepherd's crook.

"I doubt that our crossbows will do much good against them," the Anglic said in a low voice. "They crawl over rocks as if the rocks were made of velvet." We watched as

2

the huge aliens rolled eastward across the sandy beach and up over the rocks to the edge of the trampled field, waiting until the silver egg of one of our old robots floated over the tops of the wheat still growing. About two meters high with a base a meter wide, it floated on its anti-gravity plates.

As the monster approached the robot, I heard a moan from the oldest of my stepbrothers, "Handy" Mihangel, named that because he was so clever with his hands at repairing old machines or fashioning new ones—like our automatic crossbows. Using some of the lore preserved by the rectors, he had been able to re-program our old war robots and drones into farm laborers. Even as I watched, the amorphous metal of the robot's side formed into an arm with a hoe blade to chop at some weed. But the tentacles at either end of the monster caught the robot before it could complete its task.

For a moment the robot jerked about like a little fish caught in an anemone's tentacles and then the monster found its switch and deactivated it.

The monster moved back to the others slowly, holding the now quiet robot over the center of its body between two tentacles from both ends—effortlessly passing it from one pair of tentacles to the next pair on either side as the monster rolled on.

In the meantime, four of the monsters had formed a protective circle about a fatter one. The four monsters crawled about the field, sniffing anxiously. The fat one reared upward, revealing a plump pink mouth into which a second alien slid its heavy tentacles. The second monster wriggled its arms about, making loud, obscene noises. The fat monster contracted its muscles rhythmically with loud whoopings, vomiting a slick plastic sphere into the second alien's tentacles.

"Mihangel," Athvel whispered, "is that a bomb?"

"It's none I've seen in the old manuals," Mihangel replied.

3

The fat alien, now much thinner, lowered itself and raised what had been its rear, revealing a mouth at the other end. "These aliens must have several stomachs that they carry things in," the Anglic observed calmly. He was a far-traveled man even among the Folk and there was very little that could disturb his detachment, but I was beginning to feel sick.

The second monster spread the lips with two of its arms while another eased in delicately. The fat monster went into urgent convulsions and dug its bottom tentacles into the soil while the top ones intertwined with the top tentacles of the second alien. The fat monster began to sob in a grotesque parody of a human female in labor.

"This is the Sheela-na-gig for sure," whispered Cularen, the third of my stepbrothers. Cularen was as clever at conjuring the green growing things from the earth as Mihangel was at fixing machines. Creative enough in his own specialty, Cularen could be as superstitious and stubborn as the most ignorant person when dealing with anything else.

As I watched, a strange creature emerged halfway out of the slit. The creature was a bright red, made even brighter by the monster's moist fluids. The creature seemed to be kicking and fighting to get back inside. Its resistance accounted for the difficult time the monsters were having.

The other monsters spoke to the creature angrily in a series of obscene grunts and sighs, but the creature still tried to fight its way back inside. The second monster wrapped its arms determinedly about the creature's arms and lifted it kicking from the lips. The first monster, now as thin as the others, sagged slightly.

The creature was wet and slippery at first, but the second monster managed to slip off its helmet. It struggled, but the monster efficiently stripped the suit from the creature and we could see that the creature was formed like a human girl of about eight true years.

The second monster set the creature down and then

swallowed her suit, helmet, and breather pack. Then it took the plastic sphere, which it had balanced behind it all this time, and broke the sphere against the robot, coating the sides with a sticky fluid—I suppose it was some kind of sterilizer and preservative—before the monster swallowed the robot.

Athvel stood up angrily. "Now those monsters are adding thievery to vandalism."

"Looks more like a trade," the Anglic laughed with relief. "They must have found the girl child somewhere and kept her till they could return her to her own kind. Last night was probably a scouting trip." He spoke with the knowledge of years of experience. "Now they're collecting the robot as payment for their trouble."

"We need the robot more than we need one more mouth to feed." Athvel slipped the clip of poisonous darts from his crossbow and, knowing we were watching him, slapped in a clip of explosive darts. I heard the others change the clips in their crossbows as well.

"They're harmless, Lord." The Anglic crept around to join Athvel. "Look. They're making their goodbyes." He pointed at the monsters, which were stroking the creature or coiling their tentacles affectionately about her while they made cooing sounds. The Anglic held on to Athvel's arm. "Wait, Lord. You might hurt the child."

"We have to save that robot." Athvel pulled his arm free of the Anglic and started to raise his crossbow. The Anglic brought the back of his left hand hard across Athvel's face so that Athvel fell against an everblue with a loud shout.

Alarmed by Athvel's yell, our stumpies behind us began to pull at their chains with loud clinking sounds. Even as Athvel was getting to his feet, he was shouting, "Caven, Ciaran, you two are the only ones who can do anything with the stumpies! Quiet them down!"

With Caven Wilderman, a friend of ours, I ran up the hillside. The stumpies were pawing with their front legs at the chains wound around the thickest tree trunks. Parnell snuffled when he saw me and lowered his head, letting me stroke the cream-colored fur under his chin. Many of the older folk and even many of the Ships' Born, including Cularen and Mihangel, were afraid of stumpies and would hardly go near them. But stumpies, or six-legged mega-sloths, are really very gentle creatures, though they are large and imposing; for they weigh nearly three metric tons and stand nearly four meters high at the shoulder.

Even so, they respond easily to a pressure of the knees and a pull at their reins. The trick is to think of the stumpy as part of your own body—a recalcitrant part, to be sure, but a part nonetheless. If there is one thing that will make a stumpy mad, it's to confuse him. They are very much creatures of custom and very stubborn about not breaking those customs.

We almost had them calmed down when suddenly the wind changed, carrying the scent of the aliens up to us. The stumpies began to pull at their chains and they wouldn't be calmed by our hands any more. Suddenly one of the stumpies reared upwards and Caven, still holding on to its reins, was lifted into the air. He let go, landing with a jar. "The only safe place to be if they stampede is on top of one of them," he shouted to me.

The trees to which the stumpies had been chained began to tremble. Caven grabbed me by my waist and tossed me up in the air toward Parnell's back. I landed with a grunt and scrambled to the top of Parnell by grasping handfuls of fur. In the meantime, Caven had somehow climbed up one swaying tree and swung himself from a branch onto the back of his stumpy.

I managed to grab the chain bridle just as Parnell suddenly tore the tree up by its roots, rearing up to his full nine-meter length. Parnell twisted his head, the chain bridle jingling, and the double-leather reins broke in my hands.

I clutched a handful of fur in each fist, spreading myself flat against his back. For a moment the tree dangled from the chain against Parnell's belly. Then Parnell used his middle legs, digging his paws into the tree trunk. The chain snapped and the tree crashed to the ground. And Parnell plunged forward.

"Run, Lord, run," I heard Caven shout.

Athvel jumped aside barely in time as Parnell charged past. Shadowy branches whipped past us; and if an everblue loomed in front, Parnell simply threw his great bulk forward, giving a little snort each time as he shoved a tree over with his chest and shoulders. Suddenly we broke out onto the beach, heading eastward toward the fields.

The monsters, which had been making their affectionate farewells to the creature, suddenly plopped back onto the ground and rolled past me toward the sea at a good forty-five kilometers an hour. The terrified creature ran after the monsters, crying to them in their own abominable language. The monsters traveled recklessly, bounding up in the air over the rocks, not trying to control their momentum as they went into the sea, sending up giant sheets of spray. The creature dove into the water and she kept diving after them, but her lungs would force her back to the surface. It was obvious that the monsters had taken her suit away to prevent her following them.

The stumpies' peculiar humping gait, which looked so comical, was also very hard on a rider's stomach, especially if she was lying down on its hard-boned back. I crawled forward until I was astride the neck. Then I angrily grabbed hold of the chain bridle. Parnell shook his head, but I was so angry and ashamed at having lost control of him that I hung on anyway, swearing at Parnell with Da's choicest phrases. Parnell seemed shocked more by my vigor than my eloquence and he hung his head obediently, turning around toward the beach and clumping along.

The Anglic and Athvel rode up behind Caven on his

stumpy with Mihangel and Cularen half running and half being dragged as they held on to the furred sides. I shoved myself back off Parnell's shoulders and when I tried to sit up straight, I felt how sore all over I was from the pounding ride, though it had only covered a half-kilometer. Mihangel, however, was not impressed by what I'd done.

He came puffing up below me. "Da's told you never to use that kind of language," he said sternly. He was a deacon in the rectory and took his duties seriously.

"The girl will drown," the Anglic said, "unless we get her back to shore."

The creature swam easily and effortlessly in the water. I suppose all her remembered life she had been swimming inside the ship of the monsters. The monsters, though amphibious, probably preferred water. We watched her swim farther and farther away from shore, disappearing periodically as she dove after the monsters until her lungs forced her back up. We rode down slowly to the beach then and dismounted, calling to the creature to come back, but she only stared at us as if *we* were the monsters.

"I bet it's our clothes that are frightening her," the Anglic said. "Take off yours, Ciaran. Show her that we're like she is."

"I couldn't," I said.

"If you don't, I'll take your clothes off of you. Are you going to let that little child drown because of some false sense of modesty?"

"Turn your back, then, all of you." I fingered the bottom of my tunic. When they did, I jerked my tunic over my head and unpinned my kirtle so that it dropped to the ground. Then I stripped off my underwear so that I stood naked and self-conscious on the beach. The creature, in the meantime, had swum back toward shore, drawn by curiosity. She stared at me for a time, her head bobbing up and down in the waves. Finally she splashed out of the water and I could see that the creature was perfectly human.

I let her touch my hair and shoulders, but pushed her hand away when she became too personal. "No," I said.

The creature seemed startled and ran back to the water, standing with her legs braced against the pull of the surf. I tried to coax her back, using all the other Taran tongues that I knew, helped along by Athvel and the Anglic, who suggested phrases over their shoulders. But the creature remained by the edge of the sea.

"If she's spent most of her time in a suit," the Anglic finally reasoned, "she'll be used to hearing sounds over her suit radio, so she might be frightened at hearing voices so clearly."

I spoke to the girl in a whisper and the creature slapped her hands against her ribs as if to signify her understanding. As we learned later, the monsters would pound their arms against their sides in the equivalent of human clapping. The creature pointed to my tightly closed legs and loudly grunted a sentence in the monsters' barbarous tongue. Grunting, the creature tried to pry my legs apart. I shoved her away.

"No," I said firmly and tried to put my tunic back on, but the creature became annoyed and tried to snatch my clothes away.

"Here." The Anglic stripped off his leather tunic and threw it over his shoulder to me. "Put that on her."

By pantomime and insistence, I managed to get the girl into the Anglic's tunic, which made a kind of dress on her. Relieved, I put on my kirtle and tunic again. The creature pointed excitedly at the Anglic's hairy chest and motioned for him to take off his leather trousers.

But he refused. "There's no use raising more questions than we can explain at this point."

We exchanged names in the time-honored fashion of pointing to ourselves and then enunciating the sounds. The creature picked up our names after a while, but no one was able to pronounce her name.

9

The Anglic looked at her admiringly. "Until she speaks, she's a pretty enough little thing."

The creature was indeed very pretty. Her round face narrowed sharply to her chin, giving her an elfish look; and her eyes, large and round and soft, seemed to fill most of her face. She seemed unusually hairy and unkempt—not that she had a mustache or heavy body hair, but because she let her black hair grow down full and long so that it reached nearly to her buttocks. Both men and women in the Folk shaved their heads when they came of age, letting only their scalp locks grow long, or if they were among the older ones, they might shave the top of their heads, with their hair in little braids running around the head and reaching only to the shoulders. Even children kept their hair cropped short.

The Anglic put his hands behind his back for a moment. "Her suit fitted her so well, those things must have found her not too long ago. I suppose those things salvaged some life-support systems too from wherever they found her—a wrecked ship or colony. Maybe an air producer to replace the air in her breath recycler. And maybe a food machine, like a protein-bar maker. They could feed her through the little air lock on the front of her suit." The Anglic tapped a similar device on the front of the suit that was there for just such an emergency. Most suits had them.

"You seem eager to explain how she could live with those things," Athvel said grimly. "But why doesn't she remember her own kind?"

The Anglic waved both hands angrily. "How should I know? Maybe the shock of whatever catastrophe did in her family blocked any memory of a former human life. Maybe she only remembers living with those things."

Athvel's reply was lost in the muffled roar that rose in the blackened sea. The waves began to billow higher and higher, crashing on the beach. And then, far away in the deep part of the sea where the water lay calm on the surface like black glass a huge golden ring of fire appeared. The water began to bubble and the waves surged higher up the sand and then the ring of fire burst free from the water with a shrill, high, whining sound. For a moment we saw the black, fire-rimmed disk blot a small patch of stars as it hovered.

"That must be their starship," the Anglic said. "Our radar couldn't pick it up because they landed in the sea."

"Recognize the type of ship?" asked Athvel.

The Anglic shook his head. "None like I've ever seen or heard of. They're probably traders. Might wander to a thousand different stars and never make contact with the Fair Folk. Even if they did, how would they know that we're the people the Fair Folk are looking for?"

The ship began whirling faster and faster, whipping the sea beneath it into a fine spray, and then it shot upward until in the wink of an eye it was nothing more than a bright, twinkling star.

The creature pointed at the star, shouting in that same throat-tearing language as before. One series of syllables that kept being repeated over and over sounded like *Lugashkemi.*

"Forget the Lugashkemi, if that's who they were," the Anglic said gently. "You've got us now."

And the creature turned to stare at him, hearing the familiar word. "Lugashkemi, Lugashkemi," she kept repeating. And then she began to grunt in a quick, breathless way.

"What do you think she's doing now?" Athvel wondered.

"Maybe that's the way the aliens show they're sad." The Anglic scratched his cheek.

"It'd help if there were tears," Athvel said, leaning over slightly to study the girl, who was doing her best to ignore him, staring at the empty night sky.

From where they had been hiding in the fields, two men emerged, walking down to the beach to join us. One man,

11

Tuathan, was the old veteran whose holding this was. Tuathan leaned over now to his son, Tuighe, and whispered in his ear. Tuathan rarely spoke to anyone directly, for he wore a mask over the lower part of his face because his mouth had been twisted all about and the flesh hideously scarred. Whenever he spoke, his words came out twisted as well, so only his family understood him. We had not the healing powers of the Fair Folk; and since his face could not be repaired, Tuathan had asked Da if he could come to the farthest of the northern holdings, apart from everyone else. When Tuathan had finished speaking, Tuighe, a thin, bony man, turned to the rest of us. "My da thinks she's the Lady's Curse for sure, come on this, the day of Lord Athvel's birth."

Poor Athvel.

He had been born with the silver hair of his mother, Lady Daedre. It was for her that Da had broken the ancient sword oaths our ancestors had sworn so long ago to Ard-Ri, one of the greatest emperors of the Fair Folk. The Lady Daedre had been a hostage of the Fair Folk—though a finer prison no mortal ever knew, since the Fair Folk are masters of illusion. Da and his regiment, the Ninth—or the Hounds of Ard-Ri, as the Fair Folk had called them—had freed the Lady Deadre, stolen some ships and fought their way across the mightiest star empire anyone had ever known, with everybody's hand turned against them—even those of their own kin. Then in final desperation they had left known space and endured the Long Flight, seeking some hospitable world. But en route the Lady Daedre had died bearing Athvel.

When she had first seen Athvel, she would not hold him, not even touch him. She simply lay on the hard ship's bunk that was her birthbed and stared at him. "Born with his own silver helmet," she said. "And full well he will need it. He will bring death to more than me." And so saying, she died. But ever after that, Athvel was known among the Folk as the Lady's Curse, the Lord's Sorrow.

Athvel bore Tuighe's comments in silence as he usually did, never showing to anyone what he felt about the curse. But Mihangel and Cularen moved in protectively. "Hold your tongue, man," Mihangel said to Tuathan, "or I'll cut out what's left of it." Mihangel was never a tactful man when it came to protecting Athvel.

I put my hand on Mihangel's arm. "You can't turn off a man's mind as if it were some machine." He grunted, mollified.

Both Cularen and Mihangel were devoted to their stepbrother, Athvel. Though they rarely understood him, they followed him in everything, so that they were often led by him into troubles with Da. Da, the Lord of all the Folk, was not really their true da. They were both the sons of a little gunnery sergeant, Cairbry, and her husband at the time, one Red Hui. When Lady Daedre had died so tragically, it was Cairbry who'd suckled Athvel along with Cularen. And when Red Hui himself had died in one of the many battles during the Long Flight, Da had married Cairbry, who eventually gave birth to me and a younger brother, Losgann. I was twelve in true years now, one of the firstborn of this world—a Worldly, as we were called, as opposed to the Ships' Born, or Shippies. I was a stepsister to Athvel because we shared the same da, and a stepsister to Cularen and Mihangel because we shared the same mother. But all of us, no matter how tangled were the branches of our family tree, felt part of the same family that centered itself often enough on the unhappy figure of Athvel.

I nodded to Tuighe. "I'd move on with your da." He looked apprehensively at the glowering Mihangel and Cularen—both of them were big men like Red Hui, their true da. Then Tuighe touched his da's shoulder, whispering urgently in his ear. The two of them started to back away.

"Wait." Athvel stopped looking at the sea. "Every Hound of Ard-Ri has the right to speak his mind. Especially

13

one who has been such a faithful liegeman to my da." He slipped a large golden ring with a strange red-and-green stone from his finger. It had been the nose ring of an alien lord that Da had taken during the Long Flight, but Athvel had worn it on his finger. "Take this as token of our thanks." He held out the ring to Tuathan, who hesitated and then took it, bowing his head. He mumbled something to Tuighe, who translated: "You're truly one of the mighty, says my da." Smiling ironically, Athvel waved them off before they could say anything more, and together the two of them disappeared into the fields, moving toward the doom of their holding.

CulAren spat after them. "A cup of whiskey would have bought their thanks. I keep telling you that you're overly generous."

"I didn't give them the ring to *buy* their thanks. We owe everything we are to such folk as they." Athvel turned round sharply on his heel. He looked at the girl, who still clung to the Anglic. "Now. Part of my dear departed mother's curse or not," Athvel said in his usually dry way, "she's cost us dear." He looked back regretfully in the direction of the fields. "Over a half-hectare of wheat and a robot."

"What cost is a human life?" the Anglic tried to argue.

"We haven't proved she's human yet," Athvel observed. "Oh, she's human enough in form, but that proves nothing." There were more than enough records of contacts with aliens who were human in form but not within—at least as we understood humanity. And there were even more records of the star change—of lost human colonies for whom Tara and its ways were only distant memories.

"Lord," the Anglic said patiently, "I followed you and your da all these years and in all that time I've asked for no other privilege than to die for either one of you."

The Anglic's hair and beard were a pepper gray now, but in his fifties he still had the same bold, saucy way that made

14

him well liked by the Folk, who rarely took to outsiders—even those few strays of Taran stock who had sometimes crossed our path.

Properly speaking, he was not an Anglic but an Amerish, which was one of the major cultural subdialects. His far wanderings had brought him to Meneubrs, the western capital world of the Fair Folk; and, tiring of humanoid company, he had boldly walked into the streets where the Folk lived, for the Anglic had wanted to be with those of basic Taran stock again. The Anglic had thrown down his big, floppy leather hat and challenged any of us to fight him. At first no one had understood him; for though he spoke the true tongue, his accent was barbarous. He would say *dome* for *doom* and even mispronounce *Tara,* the name of the ancient mother of worlds, saying *Terra* instead in his high, drawling, nasal way. When the Folk finally understood him, no one would fight him, since it was clear that he was a man of power and of vision.

Athvel studied the face of that man now. "All that you say is true," Athvel said cautiously.

"Now I'm asking you, his son, to let this child live," the Anglic said quietly.

With a sad smile, Athvel shook his head. "Ask me something that's in my power to give you, man. A precious ring . . . a cup of whiskey." He smiled briefly. "The good of the Folk must come before even our debt to you. What if she's not human? What of the risks? As Da is always telling me, I'm to think with my head and not my heart."

"Then at least give me time to see if she's human," the Anglic argued. "At least until we get back to the holding, where the rectors can test her."

"She's witched you, Anglic, she has." Cularen moved his Earthstuff in the sign of Sane Collen. Mihangel copied him.

"You know what Da will say once I make my report." Athvel would have to call Da to cancel the alert that had been broadcast to all the holdings. (As a precaution, we had taken along a small but powerful radio.)

The Anglic looked as stubborn about the matter as my stepbrothers did. The Anglic wanted to protect the creature; they wanted to protect the Folk. But I for one was sure the creature was human; and I owed many favors to the Anglic, who had carved toys for me when I was small and then shown me how to ride and shoot when I had grown older. So if Athvel wanted the logic behind sparing the creature, I'd give it to him. I said, "Just tell Da that the aliens left something in exchange. It's inhuman to kill her if there's the chance she's human."

Caven folded his arms across his chest and cocked an eyebrow up at my brothers. "I dare any of you three to argue with the rectors' prize pupil."

Exasperated, Athvel tugged at his scalp lock. "I've tried that before and wound up agreeing that it would be best if my skin were colored purple and I had three eyes instead of two."

Caven eyed him critically. "It *would* be a bit of an improvement."

In a kinder time and place Athvel would have entered the rectory and spent all of his time lost in our books and microfilms. He looked around us unhappily and then shrugged. "Well, I suppose I have enough time on the way back to think up an explanation why I didn't make a full report to Da. But this is just postponing the inevitable."

two

I

After Athvel had radioed his brief report to Da, Mihangel and Cularen were all for riding helter-skelter back to the holding that same night. The Anglic, of course, was against it. Everyone looked to Athvel to decide. He sat uncomfortably for a time, trying to ignore all of us. Finally he shook his head. "You could have all the time in the world, Anglic," he said, sighing, "and still not be able to prove that little thing is human. Even so—" he turned to Cularen and Mihangel now—"I don't fancy riding hard all night to face Da in the morning. We'll sleep here tonight."

"Well, if that's your mind, Athvel . . ." Mihangel crouched and began to heap the trampled wheat stalks together to start a fire—we'd camped for the night on the edge of the fields. "I, for one, could do with a bit of supper. All I've had for dinner is this stuff." And he fished a piece of protein bar out of his pouch.

The creature began jabbering and pointing at it. Mihangel tossed it across the pile of wheat stalks and it landed in the dirt at her feet. She picked it up before we could dust it off and enthusiastically began to eat. "You see," Mihangel declared fervently, "nothing human could enjoy that." Having said that, he left to fetch some driftwood.

In the meantime, Cularen had knelt beside the stalks, reaching for his flint and stone to light it—we conserved on

17

everything: from rifles and ammunition to the fuel for lighting fires. "Fetch us those three cringies you killed this afternoon, will you, Caven?" Cringies were small, six-legged creatures with green fur and blunt, wedge-shaped heads. Their shortened fore- and middle-legs made them run in cringing hops.

The creature sat silent, licking the crumbs off of her dirty palms and fingers, watching in fascination and not a little distaste as we skinned and spitted the cringies. And she was utterly bewildered when, after all those elaborate preparations, we set out to "destroy" them by burning them in a fire. She was totally disgusted when we put a piece of cringy into her hands.

The Anglic and I made motions to eat it, but she shook her head suspiciously. It was only when I took a bite that she nibbled tentatively at her piece. Then she took a large bite. She almost gulped the rest of it down and then, with grease covering her mouth and hands, she began pantomiming, wanting to know what else in our surroundings she could eat. It was only with great difficulty that we discouraged her from eating leaves, dirt, and pebbles.

We also discovered that the creature was used to disposing her wastes through her suit's system, so that I had to take her into the bushes and mime the necessity of self-control. It worked, more or less.

And then the mists began to cover the hills as if the very earth were breathing. The creature, starting to shiver, began to pantomime something that the Anglic and I understood only on her sixth try, for she seemed to want to turn the thermostat up.

"Come along, then." The Anglic unfolded a spare blanket beside the fire. But it turned out she was used to crawling inside one of the Lugashkemi whenever she grew sleepy. The result was that she missed the warm, moist darkness of an alien's belly and the reassuring beat of an alien's heart. She would not stay put, but insisted on crawl-

18

ing under the same blanket as the Anglic—she would not come to mine.

That amused Athvel no end. "Be careful, Anglic. I've heard stories about taking un-housebroken puppies to bed." And he began to laugh with Mihangel, Cularen, and Caven. I might have laughed too, but I saw the strange way that the creature stared at them. She began to quiver.

"I don't think," I said carefully to the others, "she knows what you're doing. Maybe those things she was with used some other sound for laughing."

"That proves she's inhuman." Cularen jerked his head at her. "What human creature doesn't know how to laugh?"

"Like I said. Maybe she's learned to make some other sound for laughter. And anyhow who'd recognize that howl of yours for laughter except us?"

"I've a perfectly fine laugh," Cularen said, hurt.

"For a space-raid siren." Mihangel smiled good-naturedly. He almost started to laugh, but Athvel punched him in the arm.

"Hush, man. Don't start in again." Athvel smiled encouragingly toward the creature and then picked up the small leather sack of whiskey. "We'll go to the beach, where we'll bother no one."

For a long time the Anglic persisted in trying to get her to lie down in her own blanket. Each time she would sit obligingly on her blanket, but as soon as he left her, she scampered over to his blanket again. Finally the Anglic spanked her once. She accepted it stoically. That much at least the Lugashkemi had in common with humans. Then he angrily shooed her away with a motion of his hand. She just sat there staring at him with her large eyes.

The Anglic swallowed uncomfortably. "You look at me as if I were abandoning you, damn it."

"Good night, Anglic," Caven called. He had returned before the others. He rolled himself into his blanket.

The Anglic tried to do the same, but after an hour she

was still sitting, staring at him and listening to the loud chopping noises of the stumpies' jaws chewing up grass and leaves and the snoring of my stepbrothers, all of whom had come back, with the sack empty, and had promptly gone to sleep.

"I think she's afraid to go to sleep," I said.

"Damn the child." He glanced sharply at me. "Are you sure she's housebroken, Ciaran?"

"I think so, but don't hold me to it."

The Anglic glowered at me and everyone else. "I'll beat the man or girl to a pulp that dares mention this to anyone." He held up his blanket and she crawled in happily beside him. She insisted that the Anglic hold her and stroke her hair and croon wordlessly to her. She lay quiet for about half an hour and then timidly she put her arm over his chest. I suppose that since he was a solitary man he was not used to showing affection, so with bad grace he put his arm around her. The next moment she was lying against his side, but it was not until she had her ear directly over his heart that she became comfortable and fell asleep.

II

The mornings are truly the time of the One, as the rectors say; for at those times the hills and meadows seem to be reborn, taking shape from the thick mists covering their faces as if they were slowly solidifying from our dreams. And as the sun rises brighter and hotter, the mist disappears and the hills seem to grow more solid until they stand golden brown, burned by the summer sun.

I was only the second one to greet the sun. Caven Wilderman was the first—but that was as usual. Short, dark, and intense, Caven moved with the lithe grace of a cat. He had been orphaned during our first year on this world. He and my stepbrothers were close friends, or as close as Caven ever let anyone get to him: one could never tell him to do something, only ask him. And he came and went as he pleased, staying away from home for months at a time, only to reappear in the dead of night, demanding a huge supper. Of all the Shippies, he had adapted best to our new world.

He held out his battered tin cup when I joined him, and I could smell the sillow leaves steeping in the dark-green water. I sipped it briefly, savoring the warmth. "That was no kindness Athvel did the Anglic last night," Caven whispered. He nodded his head to where the Anglic and the creature lay, their foreheads touching. Their breaths, frosting in the morning air, merged into one. "It will be even harder now on the Anglic when she's taken away."

"Perhaps the rectors will say she's human." I looked at the inside of the cup, watching the leaves turn slowly in circles at its bottom.

"I doubt that." Caven began undoing the leather laces at the neck of his tunic.

"Can't you think of some way to prove she's human?" I asked Caven.

"You're the one with all the book-learning." Caven bent forward, jerking his tunic over his head. "Can't *you?*"

"I've tried. I've tried all night." I pounded my leg helplessly.

Caven straightened up. Though it was still cold, he wanted to go bare-chested already. "Even if I could, Ciaran, I'm not sure I would."

I had always thought that Caven loved all living things, so I was shocked now by his callousness. "What do you mean?"

Caven slipped the tunic sleeves around his waist and tied them tight with a jerk. "Lord Athvel will only be making trouble for himself with both your da and the Folk."

"I thought you only killed when it was *necessary,*" I said, accusingly.

Caven walked over to where the battered tin pot sat in the coals of the fire. "To my mind, any killing that will keep

21

Lord Athvel as our future leader *is* necessary." He poured some tea into another cup and squatted down beside Athvel. Caven seemed more finely tuned to the world than the rest of us. He had sensed somehow that Athvel was going to wake up—maybe by a change in Athvel's breathing, maybe by some instinct in Caven. Anyway, he was waiting when Athvel threw off his covers and stretched out his arms and yawned. When he opened his eyes, Caven held out the cup to him.

Athvel, who was used to such performances by now, accepted the cup with a nod of thanks and sipped it. He turned, nodding to me, and then saw the Anglic and the creature. He set his cup down in the dirt. "Look at that. Just like husband and wife."

Cularen and Mihangel muttered some more dire predictions when they too woke up and saw the Anglic.

The Anglic woke with a start and sat up abruptly. Self-consciously he looked at us. "Good morning, Lord."

"Good morning, Anglic. Sleep well with your little armful?"

"Don't tease him," Caven warned.

"It's all right," the Anglic said, but I knew it wasn't.

The creature woke up suddenly and sat up frightened. The Anglic had to rock her before she calmed down. It was strange to see this rough old soldier suddenly mellow. As he told me later, he was enjoying a strange new emotion. I don't think he had ever before had anyone depend on him, or trust him the way the creature did.

She was so frightened that she had an accident.

Mihangel looked at her in disgust. "She's no better than an animal," he said. He and Cularen could be sources of immense strength in times of trouble, but they could be exasperatingly stubborn in situations like this.

"Shut up," the Anglic snapped. "Or I'll shove this fist down your stupid mouth." The creature could feel his anger and she clung to him, babbling in her barbarous

22

tongue. He petted her again reassuringly, trying to keep his voice calm for her sake. "Can't you see she's like a newborn child? She's innocent, with a kind of innocence none of us will ever know."

"She's inhuman." Cularen stepped up beside Mihangel. "She should be destroyed."

"She's something to be cherished and raised with kindness."

"Why, I do believe that you're in love." Athvel grinned.

"Why, I guess so, Lord." The Anglic sounded surprised.

"So what will you call your little creature?" None of us had been able to repeat the barbarous name the aliens had given her.

"I . . . I don't know." The Anglic turned to me. "Help me, Ciaran."

Names among the Folk are vastly important. Everybody has a public name that is supposed to help guide one's future, for one is to imitate one's Taran ancestor. Secret names, of course, are exchanged only with a few and do not necessarily have to be taken from the traditions of the Folk.

"You can't think of one, surely," Caven said quickly. For the power of naming someone should be reserved for the parent. For me to help name the creature was in some large part to take responsibility for her.

I was afraid, and yet I felt sorry for the Anglic and for the creature. In a better time and place they surely would have had a more understanding group of people around them. "Call her Maeve," I said.

"Ciaran, you shouldn't have." Mihangel shook his head in reproof.

"Maeve," the Anglic repeated and smiled. "Yes, we should name her after the Elf Queen." He held her out at arm's length. "You are Maeve," he said carefully.

"Mife," she said just as carefully.

"No, no." The Anglic shook his head patiently. "Maeve."

"Maeve," the girl said with an almost funny slowness.

"A name won't be the remaking of her," grumbled Mihangel.

Cularen grunted his agreement and pointed at an everblue. "We'd ride faster if we didn't have to cut down one of those things and cart it back."

The Anglic shook his head. "You boys are forgetting why we came up here in the first place: to bring back a yule tree." Though the world was well into summer, it was yuletide by the true calendar. Leave it to the Anglic to fight for the yuletide. The first winter I remember was when I was five and the true December of Tara actually coincided with the winter of Fancyfree. We'd been hungry for a long time, since the harvests had been poor, and many of the Folk had perished from the cold and want of food. Because we hadn't as yet tamed any animals to ride, the Anglic had marched off alone into the hills and had come back dragging an everblue behind him, though he'd nearly lost his toes and fingers.

"Where's your yule spirit?" Athvel asked Cularen.

"It's a bit hard to feel in the yule spirit when the day promises to be ninety in the shade and the land itself is so brown and dry," Cularen grumbled. "I hear that yules should be cool and white."

"And what would you be knowing of white yules, Shippy?" I teased. "You never even knew what rain was before you came here."

"I know enough of snow and rain to know that I don't like it." Cularen shaded his eyes to stare up at the sky. "I'll take a hydroponics room to this any time. "There's little gentleness to this world. When it's clear, it hurts your eyes." Which was true, for the sky here burned an intense blue.

"Aye," Mihangel agreed, "or these great big brutes of storm clouds rise up from the sea and charge over the hills. And at night the chill is enough to make a man lose his teeth with chattering."

"I suppose—" Athvel hooked his thumb in his belt—

"that you'd prefer the rational, controlled, steel-walled climate of a ship?"

"Aye, that I would, man." Mihangel nodded.

"You've forgotten what recycled air was like. No matter how much the rectors tinkered, they never could quite get the stink of the waste rooms out of the air."

"Well, then, I'd take one of those worlds of the Fair Folk with all the different levels to it," Mihangel insisted stubbornly.

"Languishing in one of their prisons, without a doubt, and bewitched and bedeviled by imps and succubi and horrors such as only they could create." Athvel eyed both Mihangel and Cularen, waiting for them to try to contradict him.

"Give me a world," I said, "that has enough space for me to grow in and enough variety to interest me."

"Peace, little sister," Cularen finally said. "For this is our world, whether Mihangel and I like it or not."

Everything was a source of wonder to Maeve as we rode back, for the land was shaped with a restless eye. Even the meadowlands between the hills sweep away in great rolling waves toward the sea. Life hereabouts is an odd mixture of land and sea. For the hiss of the wind through the grain mixes with the distant murmur of the surf, and cropping the grass on the cliffsides above the sea were a few of the sheep, one of Ard-Ri's Three Gifts, mutated from some shaggy, eight-legged creatures with a rat-like snout. And sometimes at the small outlying holdings you would see the brown sea terns of this world sidle in among the chickens to steal feed. And all these strange sights and sounds we tried to explain to Maeve as best we could.

And the land would be full of surprises—secret waterfalls that sprang out at you suddenly from the shadows, or a ravine suddenly yawning in front of you and down its steep-sided throat would be a small patch of blue-green, bright

25

as a jewel. And other hills would end sharply as if some giant had cut the hill with his sword. And the wind would blow up the steep cliffsides, leaping skyward to the sun. It would be playing then, but other times the wind would blow freely over the mist-shrouded hills, and the wind would be free and wild, crying of deaths in the past and deaths to come and how each present moment brought you step by step closer to the grave.

Maeve had been excited by everything she saw in our world, but nothing excited her more than when we topped Barber's Hill in the late afternoon. Below us lay the fields scattered in bright, sharply defined patches on the land that undulated from the bay to the eastern mountain ranges as if someone were shaking out a bright patchwork quilt in the wind, and on the seaward edge of that quilt lay Da's holding. The dooms lay huddled like white drops, or sheep bunched together against the cold, and the slate houses surrounding the dooms were like the neat, angular beads of some child's trinket.

The holding proper had been built on the top of a slight hill overlooking a bay to the west. The first buildings had been some two hundred geodesic domes—to use the Anglic's words—whose frames had been cannibalized from the five ships that had brought us here. Each triangular section of glass had been made from the silica-rich mud offshore. Everyone except the Anglic had chosen panels of frosted glass. In the very center of the holding stood our own home, Doom Devlin, which was really a complex of interconnected dooms. In the center was a large doom some thirty-five meters in diameter which was the great hall, and from this radiated tunnels to six other dooms, each about seven meters in diameter, which were also connected to one another as to the great hall. These dooms in turn were connected to an outer ring of dooms. Right next to Doom Devlin stood the chapel and the rectory and school. As it was stated in the laws of the rectory, they were all built of stone. In this case, they had been built of slate which we quarried high up in the mountains to the east. The walls were of a deep, somber blue. Outside the geodesic dooms were more little houses of slate which the younger folk had built.

Da's holding was the largest of the colony, housing some thousand souls on the eastern shore of the bay. There were another thousand of the Folk scattered in small holdings to the north and still another thousand to the south. To the west of the bay was a rich fishing bank, and to the east and south lay long, narrow stretches of rich, fertile farmland. Beyond them were green hills where the sheep could graze among the great gun emplacements and the rocket batteries which we had stripped from the starships along with the radar and scanner equipment.

Da was waiting by the foot of the hill alongside the path near the long stretch of flat, glassy slag where our starships had landed. Nothing was left now of the ships, for we had stripped them completely, wasting nothing. Grass and flowers had begun to grow again in the area and even to crack some of the slick glass in places.

Da was a tall man, built along heroic proportions. He did not so much hug you as engulf you and his voice was a world-taming roar. Oh, there are details I can give. Item: he had a squarish face with a large nose. Item: he had a long blond scalp lock that was like a golden chain and a full blond beard. Item: he had steel-gray eyes. Item: he was a little over two meters tall and massed about a hundred kilos. Item: he was getting older, but his eyes still had the alertness they had had when, as a junior officer, he had conducted a thousand-kilometer raid across Wishbone. But the striking thing about him was his presence: you became more alert, more alive when Da was about. You laughed more easily when he was there. You cried more easily too. It may sound strange to say, but he brought out the humanity in people.

27

Da was a rough, blustery kind of man who reminded me more of a natural force than a man. He simply swept people up in his great gusto for life. When he was angry, he was truly, passionately angry, and when he was happy, he was passionately happy. Nor were his moods mercurial like a child's, for he was gifted with a great intelligence. He treated my brothers roughly because that was the way he had been treated and his da before him. I was never afraid of him as were so many others.

And yet, for all that, he was capable of that gentleness which one finds sometimes in big men: gentle because of their very size, afraid to hurt the smaller things. But the tragedy was that he dared to show his gentleness only to me (I imagine that he dared to show it to the Lady Daedre, the great love of his life). He seemed afraid to be gentle with anyone else, as if he thought my stepbrothers might mistake it for weakness—especially Athvel.

With Da was Losgann, little frog, at nine the youngest of my family and the happiest and lovingest. He was the only one who was my full brother. Losgann stood at attention in the kilt and tunic of the Ninth, made from one of Da's old uniforms. Losgann could be rather vain about it, insisting that it be inspection-clean. With the toy crossbow Mihangel had made for him at port arms, Losgann was doing his best to look smart beside our da.

To their left was dumpy little Prime Rector Phoil in his somber robes of gray even in this hot weather. His medallion of the rayed circle of the Right Way jingled on his chest. He was in charge of the other rectors, who preserved and perpetuated our precious knowledge of lost Tara. They were our priests, our teachers, our healers of mind and body during peacetime, and our comrades during war.

Athvel frowned when he saw Da and the Prime Rector. "It looks like an inquisition," Athvel said uneasily. "It'd be best if Ciaran went first."

My stepbrothers waited behind me as I rode on a little

ahead. When we came down to Da, I slid off Parnell, clambering down his side. I winked at Losgann, who giggled obligingly—I was more mother than sister to him. "We fetched back the tree and a new recruit for you, Da."

Da glowered up at her, a fist on either hip. "Is that what we traded a robot for? You just said the aliens left a present. You didn't say it was a creature." Athvel knew better by now than to rise to the bait. For Athvel to show any emotion before Da only provided Da with an excuse to scold his heir further. Da seemed to hold Athvel personally responsible for the death of his mother and all the disasters we had encountered since then. Da twisted his head around. "Phoil, come see the trade my stupid son made." I glanced back up at Athvel, who wore an expression of sullen defiance—like a dog that someone has tried to beat respect into and the attempt has failed. Whenever he was around Da, the expression was almost constant and yet I hardly ever saw it when Athvel was free of Da. "Fetch the child down, Anglic!" Da shouted up at him.

I turned to Parnell. "Hai, Parnell. Down."

And slowly, with a stumpy's usual economy of motion—laziness some would call it—Parnell lowered himself on his front legs. The Anglic slid off, pulling Maeve along with him.

"Come here, child." The Prime Rector motioned to her kindly. But Maeve stepped back, speaking in her abominable alien tongue which sounded so much like cursing. Alarmed, one of the younger rectors stepped in between the Prime Rector and us and started to make the sign of Sane Collen with his nine-circled star. Phoil pushed him roughly away.

"She's just protesting to us," the Anglic tried to explain. "You frightened her."

"I'm sure that's it." Phoil nodded. He turned to the younger rector. "Go off and inventory the lab supplies, why don't you?" The younger rector looked as if he wanted to

29

protest, but thought better of it. Glumly he marched back along the path toward the holding. When the young man was gone, the Prime Rector folded his hands over his stomach and studied Maeve a moment before he tried running through a dozen languages which I recognized and then a dozen more. The Prime Rector was a very learned man—even for a rector. But there was no reaction from her.

"What do you think, Phoil?" Da asked.

Phoil pursed his lips and gave a little shake of his head. "Offhand, I'd say she was human stock. Her biological age could be about eight or so, but she could really be four true years or even twenty. You know how much mankind has changed out here in the stars."

"Well, should we drown the cat?" Da asked.

The Prime Rector shrugged and crossed his arms over his chest. "That depends on how much trouble you're willing to put up with. Our people are the salt of the earth, but they're a superstitious lot—even more so since we came here. In the Unknown, you hang on to the old customs for dear life."

"Phoil, quit fan-dancing around and come to the point."

"All right. At the best, they'll think she's a witch. At the worst, they'll call her a devil."

Da tugged at his beard and sighed. "All right. Athvel, take her out and leave her somewhere over the mountains."

I put my arm around Maeve, and the Anglic jabbed his finger at Da. "You're not going to abandon this child, Lord."

"Eh? Why not?"

"She's as human as you or I."

Da said nothing. He knew the Folk better than the Anglic. And as if to support his Lord, Caven openly expressed his fear. He purposely kept his eyes away from me while he spoke from on top of his stumpy. "Anglic, we saw her born."

"She wore a spacesuit, damn your eyes," the Anglic snapped.

"Even so, she's not human," Caven went on. "If she was of human get, why didn't she recognize her own kind?"

The Anglic shrugged. "Maybe whatever catastrophe destroyed her family gave her such a shock that she forgot any human existence."

"To all intents and purposes, then, she is an alien," Da said. "And she should be treated as such. Our lives hang by a thin thread, as you well know, Anglic, but our sense of humanity hangs by an even finer thread."

The Anglic looked at all of us as if we were suddenly strangers. "I'm an old man and maybe I should be wiser because I'm older, but I'm not." He slipped his gun, a darter, from his holster. "She's under my protection."

Da glared at him. "I am the Lord and I say she is a danger to the entire holding."

The Anglic spat contemptuously. "That for your holding."

"Then think of your immortal soul, man."

"That for my soul." The Anglic spat again.

"I'll save you from yourself, then." Da beckoned to two guards who had waited in the background. "Disarm him."

The Anglic cocked his darter, breaking the CO_2 cartridge inside. It could shoot a clip of poison darts and was deadly within fifty meters. He aimed the gun at Da. "Go on," Da said—whether to the Anglic or to his guards I didn't know. The guards, though, acted as if the instruction were for them. They snatched the darter from the Anglic's hand. Things might have been left at that, but Da had to add: "I might as well do Athvel's work for him as well as his thinking. He's such a tender-hearted little thing, you know. No brain of his own."

Da was always picking on Athvel that way. Perhaps Athvel had been stung once too often. He dismounted and stepped forward before any of us could stop him. "Da!" Athvel smiled bitterly, knowing how Da hated to hear Athvel use that word—though the rest of us, including Cularen and Mihangel, were free to use it. Most of the time Athvel used *sir* or *lord* to his face. "Da, yesterday was my birthing day, after all."

Da paled a bit and the muscles about his jaw twitched. Though we celebrated the other birthing days in our family, we never did so with Athvel's because of the painful memories it brought to Da of the Lady Daedre's death. "Yes, what of it?" he demanded when he found his voice.

Though Athvel knew he was courting his own disgrace if not death, he coolly began to count upon his fingers. "Let me see, I make out some twenty-six birthing days we've never celebrated—you understand I'm just assuming that we never celebrated it when I was a baby. So let's say we count all twenty-six presents I've never received with all the presents I'll not get in the future and lump them all together into one present." With studied casualness, Athvel slid one hand under his belt. "Let the Anglic keep the creature . . . as my birthday present. There's logic for you."

Both Cularen and Mihangel dropped heavily to the ground from the back of Athvel's stumpy. The three of us placed ourselves close to Athvel should Da lose his temper. But all Da did for a moment was to scratch the back of his neck hard—almost viciously. "Don't push your luck, lad."

"Come now, Da. Surely the Lady's Curse deserves something for his time and trouble." Athvel nodded toward Da despite the fact that Phoil was frantically waving to Athvel to be silent. "Do you think bringing you sorrow, Da, comes easily?"

Da threw back his head and laughed harshly, startling Maeve. "Bah! Let the Anglic have the girl, then. She'll be the last gift from me ever and much joy may you all have of her." He motioned to Phoil. "Phoil, rig up some mum-

bo-jumbo to convince the Folk that all the bad's been exor-
cised from her."

The Anglic retrieved his darter from one of the guards.
He pushed the button that let the gas out with a hiss and
holstered it. "Come, child." The Anglic held out his hand
and Maeve took it. With the greatest dignity they could
manage, they walked past Da.

Then it was our turn for the inquisition. But Da waited
till we'd gone home, unloaded the tree and taken our stumpies back to the pen. When he had us all arranged before
him in his room, Da started. I did not think there were so
many ways of saying idiot. Athvel took it with the sullen
respectfulness of a beaten dog. Any of us would gladly have
taken the abuse, for all the Folk thought it a great shame
that Da treated Athvel so shabbily. On his own, Athvel was
quite capable and charming, but Da could only see his
faults. Da tore into Athvel until he was only six centimeters
high. Then Da turned to me. "And you, Ciaran, I counted
on you at least to have some sense."

"It's the way of humans to help their own kind," I said,
"or so it says in the rectory."

"Does it?" Da asked Phoil.

"Yes. If you bothered reading it, you'd . . ."

Da waved his hand for silence. "At any rate, it's not
proved she's human."

"She's as human as I," I said.

"I sometimes think that may also be debatable."

"I did what I thought was right, sir."

Da glowered at me for a moment, but finally broke into
a smile. "Humph. I'd sooner come between a starving dog
and its bone than between you and your duty."

"Sir," Athvel said stiffly. "May we be dismissed?"

"Yes, yes, get your ugly faces out of my sight."

"If it pleases you, sir." Athvel spun on his heel and,
followed by my other stepbrothers and Caven, crawled out

through the paneless frame that opened on the tunnel. Behind them they slammed the wooden door that was hung on the empty frame.

I straightened Losgann's tunic. "Da has his saddlesores back again, hasn't he?"

Losgann nodded. He was obviously bubbling over with questions about Maeve, but was controlling himself like a true Hound of Ard-Ri till we could be by ourselves.

I turned to Da. "That's why you haven't dared to sit down yet."

"You know me too well," Da grumbled.

"Well, if you don't get off your feet, you'll have bunions at the other end and you'll have to give audiences standing on your head."

"It might be an improvement," said Phoil, opening up his bag and taking out a jar of ointment. Grumbling, Da lay down on his bed. I took a chair and sat down beside Da while the Rector undressed him and began to rub the ointment onto his buttocks. When the Rector was finished, Da got a towel, wrapped it around his waist and stood up.

"Da, why do you have to be so hard on Athvel?"

Da scowled. "Because I'm not only his da but also the Lord, who must see that his successor is properly trained."

"But, Da—"

"Shush." He smiled. "But it's good of you to defend your brother." He stroked my hair for a moment before he went on. "I was born and raised in one of the Fair Folk's largest cities, a capital of a province but large enough to rival the imperial capital itself, for the city covered the entire world, layer after layer, shell after shell full of people. I remember the days when I was a child and had no pride, wanting only the money to buy the good things that the Fair Folk always had. I remember how all the children would wait till one of the Fair Folk passed through our ghetto—whether for pleasure or business—and then all of us would follow him until he might toss a coin or two. And how we scrambled

34

then. Even I, a Lord's son. Here at least we're free."

"And you brought your people to green hills." I tried to cheer him up.

"Aye, and for every grain of wheat we get from the hills we must cry a tear, and for every pound of game we kill we must pay a cup of blood. To my thinking, you'd still be better off in the steel hells of the Fair Folk."

We sat in silence for a moment. Da looked sad. I, Losgann, and Prime Rector Phoil were perhaps the only people he let see him that way.

three

During the next year Maeve proved to be an apt pupil for the Anglic, since she hung on his every word. She seemed so afraid of losing him that she could not bear to have him be angry with her. She also proved to be obedient, docile, and loving, but even then she never mastered the grammar of personal pronouns. She always spoke impersonally of herself and she always spoke the Common with an abominable, throat-tearing accent. And when she was angry she would lapse into the curse-like sounds of Lugashkemi.

She was utterly devoted to the Anglic, following him everywhere; and she was so insecure that she demanded his constant attention and was quite put out with him if she were not allowed to sit on his lap and pet him or if he would not touch her—for apparently the Lugashkemi often caressed and fondled one another. Though they might sound like obscene beasts, they were really quite a tactile people, perhaps even communicating in part by such touches. Maeve tolerated me, though the Anglic had to be careful not to show me any special attention or she would become jealous. And as for the other Folk, she could not have cared less if they had been blasted the next moment and carried off to the farthest recesses of Hell.

At first while the Anglic was teaching Common to Maeve, they kept apart from others, but after a month of this, when

Maeve could understand a few words, he thought it would be wise if she met children of her age by attending lessons at the rectory.

That morning I went to the Anglic's doom, following the path up into the hills, for the Anglic had built his doom apart from the others, in the northeastern hills looking down on the holding. Like the other dooms, the Anglic's home had been made from the silica-rich mud offshore. All the Folk except the Anglic had panes of frosted glass, but the Anglic had insisted on adding chemicals to his glass so that each pane had come out a different color. The rectors had warned the Anglic that it was false vanity to have such things, but, being something of a heretic, the Anglic had only laughed at them. If he had been anyone else but the Anglic, he would have been pilloried and his doom torn down, but everyone knew that he had lost none of his old skill with his weapons, so he was left alone.

"Aren't you coming with us?" I asked the Anglic when he came out in just his trousers.

"No. Wasted enough time on her," he said gruffly. "Besides, she's got to take care of herself. What'll happen to her when I'm out ranging?"

But there was a worried look in his eyes when he closed the door to his doom. Maeve could not have cared less. She took my hand and began babbling away in that throat-wrenching tongue of hers—I suppose the Anglic had explained she had to go with me.

"Oh, hush," I told her.

She shut up. That was one of the first human words she had learned. She rolled her eyes anxiously and stroked my hand, looking apologetic. There wasn't anything to do but hug her. After all, it wasn't her fault. And there was no sense in taking out my own problems on her.

She smiled instantly. Her happiness was such a changeable thing, hanging on the simple acceptance by the Anglic or by me of what she was doing. She began talking again.

37

We walked down the rows of the dooms, past the somber, staring women to the rectory. The rectors were all inside their little complex of dooms, so it was up to me to watch the other children. They had stopped playing to gather in a compact group of about sixty—the only ones who had so far managed to survive.

There were many miscarriages and many children stillborn. The gravity was slightly heavier on Fancyfree, being 1.07 Taran normal, while the older folk had grown up on worlds of about .9 Taran normal since those were the worlds that the Fair Folk had favored. And then, too, the rectors simply did not have the medicines or skills or machines to perform the wonders of the Fair Folk. And disease also took its share of the little Worldlies.

I walked straight up to them. I turned to Maeve. "Maeve, this is . . ." And I began to point and name each one. Maeve nodded to each one, dutifully trying to repeat each name. And then I looked at all of them. "And this is Maeve," I said. "My friend."

I don't know what fool it was who described children as little angels. Children are more like miniatures of adult personalities and, as in all miniatures, certain features get exaggerated. Children can be kinder than adults; they can also be much crueler. Because I was the oldest, I was accepted as their leader—my bookishness being regarded by them as one of my foibles as the Folk affectionately accepted many of Da's faults.

"Look at the hairy little beast," someone whispered. I wished that the Anglic had let me cut her hair short, but Maeve was determined to keep it full and long, though it gave her a wild, even animal appearance in the eyes of the Folk.

"Losgann," I said, "shake her hand."

"Well, if it's for you, Ciaran." Almost indulgently he took Maeve's hand and shook it.

I turned to his little friend Ardui, who was just a little

older than Losgann. "And now you, Ardui." He was afraid of Maeve but even more afraid of me. He barely touched her hand and then scampered back, rubbing his hand against his bare leg.

But none of the others would come forward. "What's the matter, Eriu?" I asked. Eriu was seven in true years and the older child of Radog Manamar. She was looking at Maeve with wide eyes. Well, so were the others; but I singled her out because Eriu had always been the most responsive to me.

"She's the Curse of the Lady, Ciaran. Oh, don't touch her."

"Don't be silly, Eriu. She's a little girl just like you."

"No!" Neven, her younger brother, shook his head solemnly. "She's the Curse of the Lady. Our da says so."

"Then your da is wrong."

"He's not," Neven retorted angrily. Neven was only six in true years.

I got just as angry as Neven. Sheep, that's what their parents were, and they were sheep's children—and lambs may be innocent, but they are also filthy, dumb little animals. "Have it *your* way then, Neven, but don't blame me if you grow green warts on your nose."

Eriu began to cry. "I don't want warts on Neven's nose."

"Ciaran!" Rector Pheodir stood in the doorway. He was a short man, his head tonsured and the long brown hair on the fringe done into a small ring of braids. There was a scar running down the left side of his face that made his smile twisted—the result of a meeting with overzealous natives. I'd heard tales about how he had singlehandedly killed three natives in his escape, and yet he was the peacefulest man among us.

"They claimed Maeve was the Curse of the Lady," I said defensively.

"That's no reason to scare them out of their wits." Pheodir picked up the blubbering Eriu and patted her back.

"Oh, now, now, chick. There'll be no warts on your brother's nose, green or otherwise. At least not that the child could cause." Eriu quieted down to just a few hiccoughs. Pheodir looked around him. "This is Maeve, our new friend. Say hello to her."

Grudgingly and timidly they said hello to Maeve. Maeve, who had been taking the whole thing in with blissful ignorance, simply smiled and said hello. Things went all right that morning. She would not leave my side, so Pheodir let her sit by me, hoping that she might pick up something, and Maeve, of course, eagerly copied everything I did, making scrawls for the algebra problems I was working out on a slate.

But then at recess we began to play tip—*tag,* as the Anglic would have called it—and that was when things began to happen. Maeve became "it" quite easily, as she did not know enough to run at first. I pantomimed to her that she was to touch someone. She did, but soon got tagged again. The children were taking advantage of her. Well, that was all right. She would learn, and she was happy enough with all of the attention. But then Neven tagged her just a bit too hard. Actually, he pushed her. She fell, scraping her knee. She sat there for a moment staring dumbly at her knee covered with dirt and blood. I don't think she had ever had a cut in her life, protected as she had been inside her suit. She began to grunt frantically in sorrow, though no tears came to her eyes—it was as if she did not know how to weep truly. But her sorrow changed quickly to anger when she found that the cut-down outfit of mine that I had given her was now torn. She had been so proud of her new clothes. Like a regular little peacock she'd been.

She began to talk to them angrily, stamping her foot, which just happened to bring her foot onto Neven's shadow. I'm sure she was scolding them, but in that alien tongue it sounded more like cursing. I knelt down beside Maeve and put my arms around her, telling her to hush, but

40

the damage had been done. The children drew away, even Losgann.

Pheodir, who must have been watching from inside, came to the doorway. "Recess is over, chicks," he said.

But Maeve wouldn't go inside, shaking her head stubbornly whenever I pointed at the door. She then pointed in the direction of the Anglic's house and dragged at my arm.

"Better take her home, Ciaran," Pheodir said. "I'll talk to the children. Bring her back tomorrow and we'll try again."

But there was no making Maeve go back to the rectory, and the Anglic said we'd wait till she got bored with him and wanted a change.

II

Besides, school was breaking up for the harvest—the gathering of Ard-Ri's Jewels. Ard-Ri's Jewels, another of the Three Gifts he presented to the Folk, was the name given to the special mutant grain that Lord Ard-Ri of the Fair Folk had his wise men create for our ancestors when they first swore sword oath to him. He did that so their garrisons on frontier worlds could raise their own food in peacetime. It was a tall plant with a head like that of true Taran wheat but whose grains had a sharper taste. The stalk itself was fibrous and could be beaten into fibers for clothing or paper if necessary.

Though it was only February by the true calendar, this world was already well into autumn. Since the gravity was heavier, it was quite uncomfortable for the older members of the Folk when they had to exert themselves, so they were usually assigned to the old fields right around the holding. The Shippies and Worldlies were sent to fields farther away. It was a good time of the year despite the hard work, especially in the evening.

Toward twilight the veterans would come back from the fields, riding in the great-wheeled stumpy carts. Here and there you would see an old uniform jacket or kirtle, carefully mended and kept up over the years, and they would be singing the old fighting songs of Ard-Ri's Hounds.

And the Shippies would come in last because they were assigned to fields farthest away from the holding. Many of the Shippies would have their fur or cloth garments cut in the pattern of the old uniform, but all wore the insignia of the Ninth as well as chevrons if they had non-com rank. And the Worldlies would be there with me, for we could help the older veterans.

This was Cularen's time of the year, for it was he rather than Da who understood the growing of green things. Even as a child, he'd had the tending of the hydroponic rooms in the flagship. During the harvest he seemed to be everywhere, shouting, singing, wielding a scythe, or gleefully calculating the yield of a field or of an orchard.

We thought that if there would be any trouble it would be at the fields on the edge of the holding and not in the very heart of our territory, so, since we were within sight of our own dooms, no one thought to post guards. There was a grove of bilbao trees off to the southeast. Thick and squat, the bilbao trees had twisted trunks like Taran banyans and their leaves were triangular, with red veins shining in the green. Since their wood was almost useless and since their roots went deep as well as sprawling over the surface, it hadn't been worthwhile to take the grove out yet. It had always been a peaceful, shady spot, and no one ever thought to check it out any more.

But somehow one of the large, furred caterpillar creatures we called fuzzies got into the grove and planted a clutch of her eggs. The first any of us knew about it was when Eriu came toward me screaming, "Fuzzies, Ciaran! Fuzzies!" She still had her basket, which spilled berries as she ran. She'd been picking the bushes that grew near the grove.

I was standing by a water bucket, a dipper in my hand. Losgann, who was beside me, happened to have taken along his little toy crossbow. He was all set to rush after the adults running toward the grove, scythes raised in their hands. I brought the dipper down hard across Losgann's wrist.

"Ow," he shouted and dropped the crossbow.

"You stay by me," I ordered. I cupped my hands over my mouth. "Worldlies! To me! Worldlies!" And the children came running from all directions. I picked up Losgann's crossbow, though what that would have done against a half-ton fuzzy I couldn't have said.

Nineteen fuzzies rolled out of the trees, great furry hoops that broke through the adults' line easily. They unrolled as they came, stretching out their two-meter-long, centipede-like bodies. They must have been new-hatched or we would have seen them before this. Their jaws unhinged and their mouths swallowed a huge swath of wheat. Then their jaws snapped shut and their mouths bulged for a moment until their contracting bodies could push the load farther back; and the moment a mouthful started back, the mouths were opened again and the jaws unhinged for another bite. A group of fuzzies could strip an entire field in no time.

"Neven. Neven," Eriu called frantically. "Where's Neven?"

"Never mind. He's about some place." I waved my hand at the Worldlies. "Fall back now. Leave room for the others to work."

"Da never retreated in battle," Losgann insisted.

"We're the reserve," I argued. Losgann didn't quite buy that, but it sounded plausible enough so that he wouldn't risk mutiny. Slowly the Worldlies backed away. Suddenly I heard a scream and Neven appeared in the field, his head

43

and shoulders jerking above the wheat. He must have tried to hide in the field when the fuzzies came out. Now he was being swallowed by one of them.

"Stay here," I said. I started forward. The adults had gotten to the other fuzzies, swiping with scythes, stones, and sticks.

I came across a bloated fuzzy—easily twice the size it had been when it first rolled into the field. A sheaf of wheat stalks and Neven's feet were just disappearing inside of its maw. I let go the entire clip of the toy crossbow, but the little darts hardly penetrated its rubbery hide. I stepped up then and began hitting the fuzzy with the toy until it broke in my hands. And then Losgann was suddenly beside me—he'd say later that he was only following my first order to him to stay by me. His dagger bounced off the fuzzy's hide. I shoved Losgann away and he fell. Suddenly the fuzzy gave a kick of its hind legs that sent its rear end arching up. It raised its mouth and caught hold of its tail lightly in its unhinged jaw. Then the legs that touched the ground gave a kick, and it started to roll away.

Two other fuzzies began rolling away from the fields. The others were already dead or dying. Athvel and Caven, churning up a cloud of dust on the path, came riding into the field on a stumpy. "Over here," I shouted to them. They swerved sharply, charging heedlessly through the field. Losgann and I started after the fuzzy. It was already halfway into the trees. I saw other men riding on stumpies plowing through the fields. They had managed to intercept the two other fuzzies, but the one with Neven reached the trees.

I paused helplessly at the edge of that dense black tangle. It was like a gigantic hedge. Athvel and Caven thumped up beside me. "Whatever got into you to charge a fuzzy by yourself?" Athvel shouted as he jumped down. Caven joined him a moment later, holding on to the reins of his nervous mount.

"Don't you know it could have eaten you in one gulp?" Caven asked angrily.

"It's got Neven," I said. "I saw it gulp poor Neven right down."

"Well, that's a different matter." Athvel picked up his com unit from his belt. "Fetch me a hand torch by aircar. And be quick."

By now the other Hounds had gathered about. Eriu and Neven's da, Radog, was all for charging in after the fuzzy, but Athvel refused to let anyone go in. "He'd take you up in two gulps," he told Radog. And Radog simply dropped his scythe, fell to his knees, and began to sob. He had tried farming his own free holding and failed. It wasn't for lack of work so much as lack of luck, I guess. Worms would attack only his crops and leave everyone else's untouched. Or a herd of toy deer would move into his fields as if his fields had signs telling them welcome. Without the help of his neighbors he would have starved. As a soldier, he was one of the best, but he had been a miserable failure as a farmer trying to make a new life on this world.

We all looked away guiltily while his brother, Ferdie, tried to quiet him—Radog's wife had died not long ago. Then the aircar came. Da himself piloted it. He jumped out of the aircar, the hand torch in both arms. "Security was your responsibility," he said to Athvel.

"I didn't think—" Athvel began.

"That's your problem. You never do." Da jerked his head at the aircar. "Get a blaster and cover me."

Da spread his legs and braced himself against the force of the hand torch. The beam, designed for the precision cutting of stone, sliced easily through the tree trunks. Chunks of wood, twigs, and branches came crashing down as he cut a hole in the grove. And there was a smoldering of wood and a few small bits of flame, but the wood was cut away too quickly for a large fire to start.

"What if you hit the fuzzy right in the spot where Neven

is?" Athvel had taken one of our valuable old blasters from the holster in the side of the aircar.

"Would you rather have me leave him in there?" Da grunted. He started forward, leaving Athvel to follow him.

"Shouldn't we go in?" Losgann asked me. He regarded himself as grownup in everything but size.

"We're too likely to get in their way." I started to brush his kirtle. "I got your uniform dirty when I pushed you."

Losgann dodged away. "I can do it." He swept his hand brusquely over the cloth.

By then Mihangel and Cularen had clomped up—they took their time on stumpies, still not used to them.

"I've ordered in some security guards," Cularen said. "We'll flush out that fuzzy and get Neven back."

"Da and Athvel already went in after them," I said.

"And you let them?" Mihangel demanded, outraged.

"I couldn't stop them."

Mihangel grunted at the justice of that. "Losgann?"

"I'm all right." He was now meticulously picking bits of grass off his tunic. "But Ciaran broke my crossbow."

"I can always make another one. Can't make a new brother."

At that moment we heard shouts from the middle of the grove and there was the smell of burning flesh.

"Da, are you all right? Athvel?" Cularen shouted into the grove.

"Yes," I heard Athvel shout from somewhere inside the forest. There was the sound of their clearing a space in the forest—I suppose they did that so they could cut the fuzzy open. They both came out a moment later covered with gore and bits of yellowish pulp that was the already partially digested wheat.

"Neven?"

"Too late," Athvel said. "But he must have suffocated before the stomach acid started dissolving him."

Da threw his hand torch disgustedly into the aircar. He

snatched the still-smoking blaster from Athvel and put it back in the side holster of the aircar as well. "You're to make arrangements for the funeral," Da said to Athvel.

"His da's here," Athvel said.

Da whirled and pounded his fist on the side of the aircar. "That wasn't a request, lad. You are to fetch back the body and build a coffin and then bury it in the cemetery where his kin want it. And you are to do all this without anyone's help."

"That's a bit unfair, Da," Mihangel said. "It could have happened to any of us. Everyone thought the wood was safe."

Da pointed at the children. "There," he said. "That's the real crop we're harvesting. Not these stupid plants."

Da took off in a screaming of rotors, leaving Athvel to stand staring at the wood and clenching and unclenching his fists. "Get me a bag or something, will you, Mihangel, like a good man?"

"Begging your pardon, Lord," said Ferdie, Radog's brother. "But we'd rather—"

"Just be thinking about your funeral plans," Athvel said wearily.

Neven, his body already half eaten by acid, his flesh sloughing off to the touch, must not have been a pleasant sight. Still Athvel fetched the body back and worked on a coffin while the rest of us finished the harvest. But in the evening, by the fires, the stories started to go about how Maeve had stepped on Neven's shadow and that was the true cause of his death. Tuathan and his son, Tuighe, were there, having come south to help with the harvest. They began to tell the Folk of Maeve's coming and their own suspicion that she was the Lady's Curse come to us through Athvel's weakness.

I kept an eye on Radog all that harvest time, but he worked and ate like an automaton. Then we finally rode back into the holding on the great, groaning, creaking, two-wheeled carts. Radog said nothing all that time, but instead marched straight to his home, where he took out his club which he grasped in the middle. The top part was of knobbed metal and the bottom was a stick part used for fending off blows.

But as soon as I saw Radog with the club, I ran to fetch Prime Rector Phoil, so that we arrived ahead of the mob at the Anglic's doom. The Anglic was perplexed. "How could anyone think Maeve could kill anybody—much less with black magic?"

Phoil scratched at his left wrist inside his large sleeve. "You have to understand him, Anglic. Radog would rather believe that there was a malign purpose behind his son's death than no purpose at all. You can fight a malign purpose. But it's hard to accept that death may have no meaning."

"Send out the Tearless One," Radog suddenly called from outside.

"You'll have to kill me first," the Anglic called back.

"Then if you'd please step outside, we can finish this quickly."

"I'll speak to him," Phoil offered.

"It'll just postpone the day." The Anglic got up and crouched by the hole. "If you please, stand away from the door first." He threw the door open, and when Radog and Ferdie and the others stood back, he crawled through the hole. Phoil followed him, but I stayed inside with Maeve, holding on to her and trying to soothe her.

"What have I done that you should harm me and my kin?" I heard Radog say.

"No harm's been done to me and no harm to you."

"That's not what I think, Anglic. I wouldn't call killing my boy no harm." And suddenly Radog blurted out: "I saved your life once, Anglic, and yet you've done this to me."

"There is no man in the regiment I would want to fight

less than you, Radog." The Anglic spoke honestly. "I remember how the Xyfa had me cornered in their temple and you cut your way through all those howling devils, and a fine piece of bayonet work that was."

"I blame no one, Anglic, not even you, not even the creature, but it's surely the Lady's Curse come to us. And yet even so we must make an end of it here and now. Or more may die."

"She's my family," the Anglic said quietly. "She's given this old man new eyes. I'm seeing a world that I never saw before."

There was the sound of flurrying arms and legs and loud panting and suddenly there was silence. Maeve let go of me and ran to the doorway before I could stop her. We could see Radog with his face in the dust and the Anglic was riding his back, twisting one of his arms behind him. "Now get this through your damn thick skull, Radog," the Anglic shouted. "I didn't kill your boy and neither did Maeve. It's this world."

But all that Radog would do was paw futilely with his free hand, trying to pull at the Anglic. Then he tried to heave himself from the ground even though the Anglic was on top of him, and finally Radog simply collapsed in the dirt. Great tears rolled down his face, streaking the dust on his cheeks.

"I'll get you, Anglic. I swear I will."

"We're shipmates, Radog. Shipmates." the Anglic insisted almost desperately.

"There's no use trying to talk the man out of it that way," Ferdie said. "Let him go, Anglic."

The Anglic looked up at Ferdie. "We're shipmates, Ferdie. We've stood back to back in lots of fights."

Ferdie was silent for a long time. Then he lifted his shoulders up and down as if there was a huge weight there. "You'd not harm any of us willingly, Anglic, but . . ."

The Anglic let go of Radog, who lay on the ground, sobbing still. Ferdie knelt beside his brother and laid his hand gently on his shoulder. "Let's go back home, Radog. Eriu's waiting."

Radog let himself be guided as if he were a child. The Anglic watched the two men stumble back down the path.

"Go on. Don't you have duties?" the Prime Rector said to the others. Guiltily they began to trickle back down the hill. The Anglic turned back to the doom. He spoke more to himself than to us. "They were my friends. How could they think I'd harm them? How?"

III

I could hear the murmur in the air as I walked back from the Anglic's into the holding. I checked out one or two things and then headed straight for the largest of the dooms and went right to Da's room.

There was a boot private outside the tunnel. He flung an arm across the doorway. "Your da's in consultation, my lady."

I ignored him and shouted through the tunnel for Da to get his trollop out of his bed. The sentry paled. A moment later there were heavy shuffling sounds and Da jerked open the door at the other end of the tunnel. He was on his knees and one hand, holding up his breeches with his other hand.

"Ciaran, one of these days I'm going to rip your lungs out and convert them into a space-raid siren."

"Radog's kinsmen and friends are gathering. They're going to burn Maeve."

"Damn." Da began to chew at his mustache thoughtfully.

"Da, you keep doing that and you won't have any mustache left."

"That's all right. Then I'll paint the whiskers in." He sighed. "Get Phoil."

I met the Prime Rector already hurrying over from the rectory. When we got back to my doom, Da was standing by the tunnel leading to his room. "They're—" I began.

"I know. I know." Impatiently, Da tucked his tunic into his breeches.

We went down the path that circled through the dooms. It was easy to find the mob. They made a noise like the low growling of a giant animal hidden somewhere in the night. We found them outside Radog's house, faces ruddy in the torchlight. They were armed. Everyone grew still, though, when Da joined them.

"Good," Da said, studying them. "I'm glad there are so many who want some exercise tonight."

Ferdie, who stood uncomfortably at the edge of the mob, fingered his corporal's chevrons unconsciously. "Exercise, sir?"

"We're going to practice a guerrilla raid," Da said. "Assemble here in full kit in ten minutes." He eyed them, waiting for some protest. He did not bother taking names; he knew everyone there. Ferdie was the first to hurry away. Then the others melted away to get their gear. They would be back, though, in ten minutes to follow Da wherever he might lead them.

I was helping Da get his own gear together when Losgann crawled into the room. His drum, which was hooked to his belt, bumped along behind him. Once inside the room, he came to attention, looking very important. Losgann had just been promoted to drummer boy and was rather pleased with himself, for he knew how vital his role was. Our communications gear was all irreplaceable, so we had gone back to the ancient devices for situations like this.

"You won't need that," Da said. "Just your riding gear."

"There are to be no signals?" Losgann asked, disappointed.

Da shook his head gently. "No. I'm just taking the boys and girls out on a little lark of twenty kilometers. By the time I'm finished with them, they'll be too bone weary to grumble."

Athvel came in that moment and with him were Cularen

51

and Mihangel as well as Phoil—I suppose he wanted to be sure that Da and Athvel stopped any argument before they came to blows.

"Did you hear what those fools wanted to do to Maeve?" Athvel asked. He almost shook with righteous indignation.

"Mihangel? Cularen?" Da asked. "Why are you here with Athvel? I thought you wanted the creature dead."

Mihangel spoke for them both. "We don't much care for the creature, but she's Athvel's gift. No one but he may take her life."

Da shut the door with his foot. "Phoil, tell them the truth."

Phoil blinked, startled. "Everything?"

"Yes. I think only the truth will satisfy them."

The Prime Rector pursed his lips unhappily. He sat down on a stool, planting a hand on either knee. "The more people that know about it, the more danger there is."

"They're my children. Not even Athvel is stupid enough to repeat what you say."

The Prime Rector gave a shrug that was so slight it was almost invisible. "We're in a race with time. Every year, every month, every day, more and more of the equipment we brought with us breaks down. But before all the equipment breaks down, we hope to become self-sufficient at least at a pre-atomic industrial level."

All of us stood in shocked silence for a moment. Awed, Losgann pressed instinctively against me and I put one arm around him. But Mihangel was the most surprised. "Pre-atomic? But that's primitive." He looked almost insulted.

"Better than a Stone Age hunter-gatherer culture—which we could easily slip down to," Phoil said smoothly, despite Mihangel's look of horror.

"Come now, man." Athvel put his foot on a chair and leaned forward. "The rectory was founded long ago to prevent just that sort of thing happening."

Phoil clasped his hands behind his back. "We're talking

about a people who by and large have wanted and gotten little change in their lives, despite the fact that they have guns now instead of stone axes. The irony, of course, is that they're likely to be back to using stone axes if we don't protect them from themselves." Phoil shook his head in a way that I hated. "The Folk were men and women selected and trained by the Taran Empire for war, and for five centuries since then we've served the Fair Folk in the same way. Only the One knows how long the Folk were soldiering before the Taran Empire was formed. Probably always.

"Our original ancestors were only garrison troops meant to watch a more or less automated way station. They weren't scientists or especially learned people, not even farmers. And our records of those ancient days when the Taran Empire fell apart and the ships stopped coming show that our ancestors suffered terribly, living without hope on that barren rock.

"It was in those days that Hywel Da called together his military officers, his political officers, his medical officers, his chaplains, and then all of his non-commissioned officers and then all of the enlisted men and women and had them write down every fact they could remember about Tara and their homeworlds and the human worlds they had visited. Then he had them write down every scrap of knowledge they could recall. When that was finished, he had them record every story, poem, limerick, and jingle. Finally he had them categorize and codify everything they had written, and that became the nucleus of the rectory—everything that makes us human. And certain men and women were set to watching over this code.

"And four generations later, when the Fair Folk discovered our ancestors, the little way station was much as it had been in Hywel Da's time. And even though the Folk have seen and done much since that time, they have been bred and trained chiefly for war. So now there's much we must learn from the books that we never had to bother about before. For instance, though we know how to make simple field repairs on a war robot, the more complex problems were always turned over to the techs." The Prime Rector held up his hands apologetically. "We can only make the Folk do so much."

I tightened my grip around Losgann. "How can you talk about being civilized when you let them do something so barbaric as to kill Maeve?"

"They're a simple people," Da snapped, "and make no mistake about it. They're capable of being generous and warm-hearted when they have some leisure time and freedom to choose, but they have no such luxuries now."

Phoil fingered the rayed circle hanging from around his neck and the light flashed from it as he toyed with the medallion. "The rectory is to protect the Folk from their own stubborn foolishness. Teaching them their letters and history is a secondary task—though important. You see, they've made Maeve into a symbol of all that's frustrated and frightened them. We have to lead them gradually to an understanding of that.

"You and I know that a blob of boneless jelly may yet share something in common with us; but you'll find few among the Folk who will admit this."

"Tell them all this," Athvel said.

Phoil smiled sadly. "Telling them and making them believe something are two different things altogether. It's a long, slow process of education to realize this." He waved his hand at us. "Four hundred years ago this kind of conversation with this many people would have been impossible."

A long silence settled in. I saw that Phoil had intimidated all the others, so I spoke up. "Da, I don't give a hoot for all this fine talk. Will you or won't you help the Anglic?"

Da rapped me lightly on the forehead in a mixture of exasperation and affection. "Of all the skulls of my children, this is the hardest." Da's valet brought in his journey bag—mostly liquid supplies fresh from Ewen Cai's still. He strapped on his pistol belt, grunting when he found it was uncomfortable at its old length. He looked down, grumbling, at his belt buckle. "The leather must be shrinking. I'm going to have some new holes punched in this when I get back. Are you ready, Losgann?"

Suddenly embarrassed at being held by me, Losgann roughly shook free. "Yes, Da."

"Let's go, then." Da hoisted his gear and journey bag to one shoulder and nodded to Losgann to go in front of him. As Da was crawling through the doorway, he glanced back at us. "If I really wanted to help the Anglic, I would slit her throat. That's the only way to end his troubles now."

four

I

Over the next six true years the Anglic went ranging often and he took Maeve along with him—which was fine with the Folk: the farther and longer away, the better. And when the Anglic returned to the holding, he rarely stirred from his doom, staying inside with Maeve to dictate his reports on what he had seen while ranging and cataloguing the specimens he'd gathered.

I saw what I could of them, but between my own duties and studies and their frequent trips, those meetings were few though always happy ones.

And then in my eighteenth year I had to go through boot camp and then on assignment with a squad of boots to one of the outpost holdings, working on one of the labor projects. Strange to say, Caven's ranging brought him often by the outpost, so I wasn't without news of home. He even brought me a little pet, a chirpy, which I called Yeats. He was a small, furry, six-legged animal with a squat, bulbous head and a face that looked as if it'd been squashed flat, but he was capable of some fine singing, most of which he had learned from Caven as Caven had ridden back from the eastern mountains. Yeats caused a great deal of teasing from the other boots, which I resented, since Caven had always been like a foster brother to me. I wasn't sure what all the visits and the present of the chirpy meant, but I doubt if Caven himself knew right then.

But one spring day when I was nineteen in true years and had returned to the holding to take up my career studies in botany, I went down to the beach as I often did. It had become one of my small pleasures to wash the long hair of my scalp lock in the water of one of the tidepools by the beach which a type of seasonal plankton scented like perfume. In the twilight before sunrise I liked to watch my reflection on the still surface shimmering like a ghost over the softly luminescent crabs and anemones. I would look at myself for a long time and then suddenly shake my wet hair so that the drops fell like rain, shattering my image into a hundred bits of colored light.

Losgann accompanied me down to the beach so he could take his morning swim. Though he was only sixteen in true years, he had already become rather vain about his dress and grooming. He was a fine sight that morning, for he was entering the prime of his manhood, with his blond hair combed and his little bit of a mustache—hardly more than a downy fuzz now, though it gave promise of being as fine as Da's—and wearing a tunic and kirtle made from one of the few bolts of plaid cloth we had left. Half a head taller than me, he was the prettiest and fairest and most well-spoken of the Devlins; and the Folk often saw in him the promise of better times on this world, for he was a Worldly.

But as we walked down the rocks toward the tidepool, I saw a very disheveled Caven and two of the watch who patrolled the entire holding. They stood on the sandy beach below the rocks where we were.

"Now, what do you suppose that's all about?" Losgann wondered.

"Some mischief Caven's been in, most likely. It's nothing you need to know about. You come by such fancies naturally enough. It's in the blood."

But Losgann slung his towel over his shoulder. "It looks a bit more serious than mischief." He started down toward the beach. For the thousandth time I wished he hadn't become the darling of the entire holding, for among other things he also gave promise of being the proudest and most headstrong of our family—which took some doing.

I knelt by the pool and was spreading out my things when I heard Losgann scramble back up the rocks to me. "It *is* serious, Ciaran," he said. "Caven badly needs your help."

I looked down at the beach. Caven beckoned to me when he saw me looking at him. He seemed worried, but he tried to put on a smile for the two watchmen as I joined them on the sand. "Here's the Lord's daughter herself and a Worldly," he said, trying to sound at ease. "She'll tell you the truth even if you don't believe me. It's widely known how clever she is."

One of the watchmen slid off his furred cap and nudged the other to do so, murmuring, "Herself's no longer a childer." The other took off his cap as well.

By now I'd developed several kinds of voices, and I spoke now in the voice I used when going over the accounts of the household. None of my brothers would do them and Da had dumped the accounting into my lap almost as soon as I could count. "What seems to be the trouble here?"

One of the watchmen pointed with his crossbow. "There's tracks of a childer here coming down from the doom." Then he pointed at the spot where he was standing. "And they end here where the slide marks start toward the sea." The tide was rising and had almost washed the slide marks away, but there was a broad groove about a meter wide leading up from the sea, and on either side of the groove were smaller, rope-like marks.

The second watchman nodded. "I seen slide marks like that before when I saw some Seademons."

"It's like . . . like . . . the childer changed into a Seademon," added the first watchman. Afraid, they both looked to me, the Lord's daughter, to put away their fears.

Caven laughed right then, giving me my cue.

I'm afraid I was going to betray their trust. "The tracks have just gotten mixed up," I said. "Some child got out of its doom or cottage and went for a late-night swim. Probably came out in those rocks over there. And those other marks were made by some Seademon that got curious and snuffled along the child's tracks.

"Well, having Seademons right in the heart of our holding is bad enough," I said. "We should set a watch down here all the time. I'll talk to Da." I got the names of the two men so they could receive a commendation for alertness. They smiled, reassured finally, and went walking off to report and go to sleep.

Losgann waited until they were far into the holding. "Do you think they believed you?" he asked me.

"Why shouldn't they?" I asked innocently enough.

He began to dig his heel in the sand until the last of the Seademon tracks had been destroyed. "Because your harmless little tale was as preposterous as their superstitious one." The surging tide swept about his ankles, erasing even his handiwork, or rather his footwork. Losgann turned now to Caven. "Do you think they believed Ciaran?"

Caven glanced at me. I sighed and nodded. Losgann was a bit too clever to hide things from. "Those two . . ." Caven laughed again. "They're training to be ballistics computer men. All they really know is their precious tracking computers." Caven studied me. "What are you thinking?"

There was only one child who might be down here at night and that was Maeve, who had arrived back in the holding the other day after another ranging trip with the Anglic. "I think we'd best find Athvel and then have a talk with the Anglic."

"I'm going too," Losgann insisted. "You'll not be leaving me out of this."

"You'll be quiet, though?" When he nodded, I said to Caven: "Where's Athvel, then?"

"I know where he is," Caven said quickly. "I'll fetch him."

"Carousing all night?" In the last few years some escapades of Athvel's had raised the eyebrows of many of the Folk who were used to tolerating high spirits in their Lords.

"He has a family tradition to keep." Caven shrugged. It's said that in his youth Da was the same way as Athvel.

"And you?" I asked.

"You may run the doom and your da and your family, but not me."

The morning sun shone through the panes of the doom, so that it seemed to burn and hold the light inside like a multi-colored jewel. The Anglic was outside carving a small statue of the Fair Folk as he often did, for he traded such things to others as toys for their children in exchange for sewing or other chores to be done for him. He smiled, pleased. "Ciaran! Just the one we wanted to see." He called to Maeve inside their doom. "Ciaran is here. Find her welcome-home present."

As we had arranged already, the others kept the Anglic outside for a few moments so I could speak with Maeve. When they crawled through the entrance later, I was flushed and angry and standing apart while Maeve was sitting puzzled and a little hurt. But she picked up when she saw the others, becoming as happy as a puppy.

Athvel, Caven, and Losgann gathered around me. "Ciaran, what's wrong?" Losgann whispered.

"Nothing," I snapped.

In the meantime, the Anglic was waving his hand at Maeve. "Go on, girl. What're you waiting for? Fetch out Ciaran's present." Out of a chest she took something wrapped in cloth. She held it out, looking at me shyly. I took it with a nod, trying to forget what had happened.

I unwrapped it and, despite myself, said a little surprised "Oh!"

Maeve laughed. "Maeve knew Ciaran would like it."

"Yes, you did, girl."

There on my hands lay the most delicate seashell I had ever seen. In fact, I had never seen one like it. It had fine spines all up and down its surface and each was a different iridescent color. I turned it this way and that. It seemed more like a star; and its wall was paper thin. "I've never seen its like."

"We found it on the beach of a northern bay," the Anglic said.

"But there's no animal like this on the coast."

"Oh, washed up from the sea bottom, I guess."

"We've found other things too," Maeve said.

I looked around. The Anglic's walls were covered with strange trophies. Others were on the table, waiting to be mounted later: more shells, weird sponges and fishes.

Athvel took down one of the new decorations from the wall. It was the oddest fish I'd ever seen. Its insides had been cleaned out and it had been preserved with some kind of lacquer.

"Does the Lord like that?" Maeve asked. "The Anglic and Maeve found it on the beach and preserved it."

"You've a rare eye." Athvel handled it gingerly. "And even rarer luck. For no one else has found the likes of this or any of these others." Athvel looked around the room at the other specimens.

"Maeve and the Anglic can find some for you too," Maeve offered innocently.

"At what cost?" Athvel asked.

I examined the fish Athvel had handed to me. "Anglic, this must be a benthic fish—a fish that lives down deep in the sea. That's why it has all these extra fins and so much surface. And the gas bladders too. That's to help it float. And look at these eyes, they're atrophied."

"You don't say," the Anglic laughed. Laughter no longer bothered Maeve. "Well, it must have wandered too far

61

up in the night, for it came to my hook."

Losgann had been studying the fish over my shoulder. "No fish would ever wander that far up. They can tell by the pressure and salinity where their natural level is."

"Well, how did it get up there, then?" The Anglic laughed again. It sounded a bit forced now. "Not everything is in the rectors' library."

"It could have been driven," I said. "Couldn't it have, Maeve?"

"That's impossible," Maeve said.

"No, not if the Seademons liked you. And they do like you, don't they, Maeve?" It was her pretended innocence that got to me.

"No, no. Maeve does not know anything," Maeve said.

"You're lying." I dropped the shell and it broke. I grabbed Maeve and began to shake her until the Anglic pushed me away roughly. I sprawled on the ground. The Anglic was panting.

"Then you tell us, Anglic," I said. "What does she do at night? What does she do?"

The Anglic flushed angrily. "Get out," he said. "Get out and never come back." And then his arms went around Maeve and he tried to comfort her. "There, there, child," he soothed her, stroking her back.

I signed to the others and we left.

The four of us walked down to the beach together by silent agreement, stopping at a spot where we could not be overheard.

"What happened up there between you and Maeve before we came in?" Athvel demanded.

"Nothing I can talk about," I said.

Athvel hooked a thumb in his belt and sighed. "Much as it hurts me to say it, Da was right. She's more than an ordinary girl."

"The tracks only prove that a Seademon came to our beach," I argued. "Maybe she went for a midnight swim and when she came back, she came in where the surf's gentle on that shingly part of the beach near the rocks. And then a curious Seademon simply sniffed the tracks."

"There's a great many if's to that idea." Athvel smiled. "Da is always shouting at me to prepare for the worst and I think we should." Athvel considered the surf for a time. "Maeve's told the Anglic that the Lugashkemi were traders."

"Aye, but she's said little more about her past or about what they were doing on this world."

"Let's suppose," Athvel went on, "that Fancyfree was on the Lugashkemi's regular trade routes."

"That's assuming that they had someone to trade with . . . like the Seademons," Losgann said.

"I said we'd think about the worst." Athvel slipped his hand away from his belt and scratched at his chin. "So if Maeve spoke Lugashkemi to the Seademons, they'd recognize the language and make contact. Maybe the Lugashkemi even traded with the Seademons before they inspected us so that Maeve and the Seademons knew one another already at least on sight."

"Maybe the Seademons are just animals," Caven offered. "They might have become curious about her if she's been swimming. None of us swims as well as she does. Maybe she's made them into pets."

"But in either case the Seademon rookery is over a hundred kilometers away," I said.

Caven pursed his lips. "Say they can swim fifty kilometers for two true hours. Anything's possible, for we really have no idea what they can do."

Athvel faced directly into the strong southwest wind and he threw back his head, letting his long, unbraided silver hair stream away. Then he smiled in his odd way—as if Athvel knew some private joke about the universe that no one else knew. "You know, Ciaran, I've a mind to find that out, and when I've all the answers, it's only then I'll go to

Da, and won't he be disappointed when he can't find fault with me?"

"More watch must be kept here," I said.

"Oh, aye." Athvel rounded on his heel. "You can certainly tell Da about the Seademon tracks on the beach."

Caven grinned. "Aye. Ciaran was just saying how bloated you've been getting."

"Did she, now? And what of that paunch on you, Caven?"

"I suppose a hunting trip to the south would do us both a bit of good."

Athvel winked at us. "We just won't tell Da how far south we're going or what we're really hunting."

"And Mihangel? Cularen?" I asked Athvel. "Will you tell them?"

"Cularen's busy with his planting. And Mihangel's to be married in three months. This is no time to be calling them away. Besides, they haven't the heart for this sort of thing."

"What about me?" Losgann asked anxiously.

Athvel crossed his arms, amused. "You're a bit young, aren't you?"

"I killed three skulkers last winter," Losgann declared. "I can hold my own."

"We'll need someone to hold the stumpies' reins, I suppose."

"Athvel," I protested, "you can't be thinking of taking Losgann."

Athvel looked down at me calmly. "He's old enough to show his true mettle."

Losgann put his hands on my arms and moved me gently but firmly back a step away from him. "It's time I let go of your hand, big sister."

"It takes more than a mustache to make a man," I grumbled. "I'd better go too."

Athvel gave my scalp lock a little tug. "You've this now too. Or have you forgotten? You're of age now, so you're

64

to begin working with your own company." Actually, my adjutant, Captain Ian, would run the day-to-day routine for me; but my command was no honorary one. I would be responsible for it in general and lead it into battle with the Fair Folk should that day ever come. I had always wanted my own command, but now I would gladly have given it up.

Losgann smiled his most charming smile. "And who would handle Da? Not me. Not Caven, nor Athvel."

Athvel gave a laugh and hugged me. "You've the most dangerous mission of us all, I think."

I could not go with them without making Da suspicious, I was reconciled to that. "Take care." I returned his hug and pecked him on the cheek. "And you—" I pulled Losgann's proud head down so I could kiss him as well—"you obey every word of Athvel's." But when I would have pecked Caven, he held me off for a moment.

"It will be a long time before I'll see you again, Ciaran," he said.

"So?"

"This is more like what I had in mind," Caven said. And before I or Athvel could say anything, Caven had slipped his arms around me and kissed me—and not like a friend of the family. And there was many a girl in the holding who'd taken a fancy to his dark looks and his tunic and kirtle of deep, rich furs and his wild ways, but I wasn't any little flutter-by to be caught by looks or clothes or manners; for I was a Devlin, after all.

When he let go of me, he sighed. "There, it's done. Now you know you have my heart."

I was flustered, but I was not about to show it. "Aye, but Kate Milligan has the rest."

"An infatuation." Athvel waved his hand airily.

"That's not what *she* says." I rounded then on Athvel and Losgann. "Why didn't you defend my honor?"

"You've told us often enough how you're capable of taking care of your own self."

I gave up then and laughed. "Remember, Athvel, Mihangel's to be married in three months."

"Aye," Athvel laughed. "We'll be back long before that. I'll be there at the ceremony to hold the brave man's hand."

But Athvel came home sooner than he or any of us expected.

II

They came back in a month, the three of them gaunt and pale and with a wild look in their eyes—as if they had just had some bout with the Devil himself. Caven dismounted first, taking up not only his reins and the reins of the riderless stumpy, but those of Athvel's stumpy as well, and tied them to iron rings on the pillar. Then Caven urged Athvel's beast to kneel so Losgann, who had been holding Athvel, could lower him to the ground. Athvel tried to stand, but crumpled up like a rag doll, and Caven gathered him up in his arms and carried him into the doom as though Athvel were only a little child.

Caven laid Athvel down on a wooden bench. "Fetch the rectors," he said to me. "He's lost a terrible lot of blood from a wound we had to cauterize. And he's been so feverish, I was afraid to travel."

I grabbed hold of a man, one of the boots who was obligated to serve in the doom as part of his training. "Don't just stand there gawking. Do as he says." I turned to another boot and told her to fetch me some hot water and a towel. Then I knelt beside the bench.

"Why didn't you send word?"

Athvel licked his blistered lips and smiled weakly. "You know Da. He would have fetched me back in a litter like some precious old sow."

When they brought the basin of hot water, I had them set it down on the floor next to me. Athvel lifted his head slightly so I would have an easier time unwinding the ban-

dage that ran around his head. I couldn't help a little gasp.
A terrible scar ran from his jaw, perilously close to his left
eye and up to his forehead.

Athvel saw me staring. "Is it so ugly?" he asked.

Actually, it wasn't. It did not so much ruin as enhance his
looks, for it seemed to collect all the strength and fire in his
face. But I didn't know how to tell him that, so instead I
began to wash the wound. When I had finished winding a
clean bandage around his head, I sat back on my haunches.
"Who or what did this to you?"

Athvel turned his face away. "Dismiss everyone."

I nodded to the boots and regular servants who stood
about. They left, though reluctantly, down the corridors
that ran away from the central doom like spokes.

"It was Maeve who did this," Caven said quietly.

"But that's impossible. When she hasn't been in the
holding, she's been to the north with the Anglic."

Caven spread his hands. "I know what I saw."

Phoil burst through the main entrance the next moment
with Pheodir in tow, staggering under the medical chest.
Da followed them, along with a grim Mihangel and Cularen.

Athvel sat up slowly. He tried to wave Phoil and Pheodir
away. "My wound's healed already." He looked at Da. "I've
things of great import to tell you."

I could see Da's chest swell up. It was as if he would burst.
"You have things to say to me?!!!"

Da always did have a flair for languages, so that he used
several of them, both well-known and obscure ones, to
curse Athvel for being so reckless, disobedient, and so on.

I suddenly grabbed Da's arm and twisted it slightly so
that he was forced to turn away from Athvel. Da was so
shocked that he did nothing, merely stared at me in amaze-
ment as he rubbed his arm when I let go.

"Da, I know you're nearly mad with worry. Don't act as
if you're about to drive Athvel away."

Da wagged his finger at me, jutting out his beard. "Don't you ever do that again, young lady. I'm your commanding officer besides being your da." But then he smiled and put a fist on either hip. "Hah, it's good to have a peacemaker at home, though. Let's go to my room."

Da poured them drinks of whiskey with his own hands before he would let them report.

They had ridden south to where the world spits up black mountains, sharp-peaked as fangs. Since Fancyfree was in its glacial period the sea level had dropped some thirty meters exposing a great deal of Seademon territory that was ordinarily part of the dark depths of the sea. Because the Seademons hated the light, only a few of the hardiest might dare the upper waters in the daytime. Athvel and the others were fairly safe as long as they went down into the sea during the daytime and stayed in regions which were fairly clear and well lit. With an adaption to our breather packs and with the addition of fins and weight belts, we had been able to convert our old spacesuits for diving, since the principle was the same: to keep a pressurized atmosphere around the wearer.

Athvel paused for another sip of whiskey. Then he began again. "About fifty meters down we found some deep gullies in which the Seademons expose their dead until the carrion fish and crabs eat the rotting flesh. The bodies were there by the hundreds, piled on top of the old skeletons. It was a ghastly sight: the bodies lying in piles and the fish darting about in swarms, looking like giant silver ghosts dissolving and materializing over and over, while the sea surged and the crabs rattled the bones together."

"So they believe in burial customs," Da said musingly.

"Aye, and more. We found a temple." Athvel paused to let that sink in. "And we found cromlechs—huge slabs of granite, maybe three meters high, set into the continental slope. Don't ask me how they cut them off from the cliff and

68

kept the barnacles from gathering. But they're there and they had these curious pictures. Giant Seademons with tiny baby Seademons sucking at their bodies.

"And the temple itself was a ring of stones made of huge slabs standing on end, and crowning these slabs were other ones. And within the temple we found a big slab worn away in the middle so there was a bowl-shaped hollow. In one corner we found the skulls of megasloths and some other land animals we didn't recognize, but they looked old, maybe even of fossil age—like they had been there for eons. All the skulls were staved in. And then we saw that there were more skulls lined up in the open spaces between the stones.

"And we found one more thing. Show them, Caven," Athvel said.

Caven took an object out of his pouch and held it out for us to see. It was a Seademon mask made out of small chips of jade glued to something, perhaps leather. The mask was too small and of the wrong shape for a Seademon. But it was about the right size for a human face, though if it were used under the sea it would have to be tied over a helmet and the wearer would be almost blind.

"We heard drums that evening. We had camped way up on a mountain and the mist had covered everything, but we thought we heard snuffling sounds and groans out there in the dark. It raised the hackles of our necks, let me tell you. From the sea we could hear a booming sound. Hollow logs, maybe. And though we were high up on a cliffside, I swear we heard a distant scrape-scrape-scrape of hide on rock—like Seademons drawing themselves over the rocks. We doused the fire and I put on a suit and helmet to use the infrared scanner, but I couldn't see anything. Caven and Losgann put on their outfits too and we both stood watch the rest of that night."

"How could they get on land?" Da asked skeptically.

"We were near the Devil's Eyes," Athvel said.

69

The Devil's Eyes were a peculiar formation, the result of a war long ago between the land and the sea during another glacial age when the mountains here had been lower and the salt sea had eaten and nibbled at the rock, forming chimneys and caves that honeycombed the Wailing Mountains. And then at some unknown and distant time the mountains had reared up suddenly, lifting their heads high over the sea—even higher now that it was another glacial age. But half a kilometer inland within the Wailing Mountains lay the Eyes in deep valleys, valleys so deep they were only a half-meter above sea level. And the salt water of the holes looked like black mirror pools.

For the longest time we thought nothing grew in them or near them. But once, during the terrible winter of our second worldly year here, there was a terrible famine—a drought, you see. And many families went ranging for food, and one such family—a father, mother, and son—did go into the Devil's Eyes and they found growing near the edge of one of them some of the native wheat. It was tougher and harder, but it was edible. Perhaps it was the soil or some fungus in the area, but the wheat was strong in ergot, a natural form of hallucinogen. The entire family went mad, the son telling us later how his da and ma changed into monsters and crawled into the pool to drown. Some of their kin dove into the Eye and found strange fish in the black water—fish with large, staring eyes, thin of body and long of jaw with glowing whiskers and horns. All of them dancing and gleaming and fighting. The divers left the Eye quickly.

And it was said afterward that if you let your reflection fall upon the surface of an Eye, the demons inside the pool would catch it and with it catch your soul, so that when you died, you would haunt that particular Eye forever. And hunters who ventured into the Wailing Mountains thereabouts had a way of breaking an arm or a rib or even disappearing, so that eventually all men and women shunned the place.

"The Seademons," Athvel said, "couldn't know we were there, for we stayed put in our cave and kept the stumpies in the back at night. We took them out to graze only during the day. I suppose the Seademons were feeling secure, for after three nights we heard the singing, strange and high and wild. It was beautiful and yet strange. The tonal structure was different and the sounds . . . the sounds ought to have torn a human throat apart. Do you understand?"

I nodded. "I've heard Maeve sing."

"We had to know. We had to see, so the three of us donned our suits and helmets and crept out into the night. We followed the song until we came to this one Devil's Eye which lay between the western spurs of a hill. This Eye was large, almost a perfect circle about fifty meters in diameter. But the Eye itself was funnel-shaped, tapering sharply to only ten meters in width a hundred meters down in the pool. The peculiar shape of the valley made each sound echo until one had to become sensitive to one's own body —each movement, each breath seemed exaggerated in the silence.

"We crept to the top of the hill and looked down to see Maeve sitting beside the Eye, naked, combing out her long black hair and singing to herself—a strange song in no language which either of us knew and whose sounds were not meant for a human throat. About her, lying around the rim of the Devil's Eye, were Seademons, long, conic bodies lying flat on the rocks, dangling their tentacles in the water, lazy-like.

"In the tentacles of some were fireworms. Those coral worms which group together on ropes or cables or any surface—in this case, on sticks of driftwood. The fireworms gleamed with a soft, ghostly light, and on the surface of the pool hundreds of tiny butterfly-like snails shone. I listened

71

to her for as long as I could, but then I had to talk to her, so I took off my helmet and stood up and the pebbles rattled down the hillside, and the hill and spurs magnified the sound into an ominous rumble.

"Maeve stood up like a startled bird, holding the small bundle that was her diving suit.

" 'Wait!' I shouted. She clapped her hands and immediately the Seademons hid the fireworms within their own tentacles so that it was dark. Neither of our moons was in the sky, so I snapped on my wrist lamp and plunged down the slope, bruising and cutting myself on the rocks. The clatter of falling rocks and pebbles rose to a deafening roar. In my beam of light I could just make out Maeve struggling into her suit.

"She had gotten both legs into it when I grabbed her by the waist. 'No, don't run.' She was small but surprisingly strong, and both of us tumbled into the water. Using her helmet like a club, she hit me frantically about the head and shoulders, but I managed to get hold of her and made her drop her helmet. That was when she took out her knife—just a flake of obsidian, really, but razor sharp.

"It gleamed in my lamplight. She meant to take out my eyes, but I ducked in time and felt the point cut a searing line down the side of my face. Blood spurted into my eyes and, blinded, I let go of her and kicked toward the shore. I groped for the rocky side, but my hands were too slippery. I thought I would drown, but then I heard a low word of command and felt myself encased by strong, tight coils and hoisted bodily from the water onto the rocks.

"I managed to blink the blood from my eyes and saw the largest Seademon. Its right eye had been torn in some fight long ago so it had a perpetual stare. Maeve was swimming cautiously toward the edge of the Devil's Eye. Another Seademon had resurfaced and it floated efficiently to her side. The tentacles of the Seademon held her helmet, but she refused to take it at first. Instead she climbed out of the

72

black water and took out a bandage roll from the medical kit in her own suit. While the Seademon held me, she cleaned the cut with antiseptic and then placed the bandage around my head. The material clung with a soft sucking sound.

"She looked down on me one last time and then took her helmet from the Seademon. She did not put it on before she dove into the sea. She did not come back. The one-eyed Seademon released me and jetted out toward the center of the Eye, as if daring me to come into the water again. It spread its tentacles so that the mouths gaped wide, revealing needle-fine teeth inside. A dart from Caven's crossbow splashed the water and it dove, the black water swallowing it up."

"You were right in the middle of the Seademons," Caven said, "so I couldn't shoot before."

"Never mind that," Athvel said and continued. "I shone my light on the water so we could search the Eye. It sent shivers up my spine to look at the black water so still and deep. Somewhere down below, Maeve was accomplishing the difficult task of putting on her suit underwater. Suddenly bubbles rose to the surface. She must have managed to flush the water out of her suit. There was no wind, but suddenly the water rippled mysteriously near the center of the Eye, so we knew the Seademons waited and watched, perhaps hoping we would come closer to the edge so they could strike.

"I found this the next morning by the Eye." Athvel held out a crawler-shell comb. Da turned it over in his hands. He glanced at me, raising one eyebrow. As much as it hurt me to do it, I nodded. It was Maeve's comb all right, for no one but the Anglic could carve such fine designs on a comb and I had seen the very same comb in Maeve's hands often.

Da tapped the palm of his hand with the comb. "This temple. How do you know it wasn't built by some other race and the Seademons simply playing around there?"

73

"As for that, we can't say for sure without further investigation, but the temple was of a size and shape for them," Athvel said.

"Damn it." Da threw the comb down. "Why didn't you come and tell me of your suspicions?"

"Because you'd have shouted at us for going off halfcocked with no proof." I spoke before Athvel could. Da would not stay as angry if I were involved in the matter along with Athvel.

"Aye," Losgann agreed quietly, "you've always expected more of Athvel."

Da mulled that over for a bit, gaining control of himself. Then he jerked his head at us. "Well, what do you suggest we do about the Seademons and Maeve? I'm open to suggestions."

"Lord," Caven said, "the Tearless One must be destroyed before she brings ruin to us all." Caven was doing Athvel's talking for him—Da would be less critical if it came from someone else.

Even so, I turned in shock and rage to look at Caven, but he steadfastly ignored me, looking only at Da. I turned to Da as well. "Before you could kill Maeve, the Anglic would kill not a few of the Folk."

Caven pressed his lips tightly as if he were swallowing his words, but Da gave him no chance. "Speak your mind, man," Da snapped. "This is a council."

Caven glanced at me helplessly and then went on. "It's best the Anglic were to die too—not because I wish him dead but because I would save him from greater sorrow."

"He's right, you know, Ciaran," Athvel said gently. "We should."

I appealed to Da. "Don't you see? If we kill Maeve, we'd be throwing away a priceless opportunity to contact the Seademons. Maybe we could even become allies."

"I'd sooner stick my foot into a skulker's mouth," Caven

74

said. "Most likely she's already told them of our weaknesses."

"What would Maeve know of war?" I leaned forward urgently in my chair. "We can't turn our backs on anything that might lead to a channel between the two races."

"And you—" Da turned his gaze toward Losgann— "what do you think?"

Losgann grew pale, but he returned Da's look steadily. "I agree with Ciaran."

"You can't be meaning that when she's struck Athvel," Cularen protested.

Mihangel nodded. "She must pay for that."

Da slumped in his chair, looking as if he bore three tons on his shoulders. "For the moment, no real harm's been done, so we might as well try to use Maeve, but if at any time there's the hint of danger for the Folk, she'll have to go and the Anglic with her."

Athvel's face had grown still, refusing to show any sign of disappointment or resentment. Cularen and Mihangel simply stared in disbelief.

"You'll find no treachery in Maeve," I said. "She won't be friendly to your face and plot your death behind your back." I glanced at Caven then. I couldn't help it, for he had been the last one I expected to go against me.

"I won't afflict you with my presence any more." Caven rose from the chair he'd been sitting in. He turned stiffly to Da. "By your leave, Lord, I've a mind to search the eastern wilderness beyond the mountains. This might be an opportune moment."

Athvel glanced unhappily at me and then back at Caven. The council had had side effects he had not expected. "A night's rest—"

"Will do no good," I said. Hurt, I wanted to hurt.

"Woman, your tongue can cut finer and quicker than the

finest New Bethlehem steel, but remember it can cut two ways," said Athvel.

"Excuse me, Da," I said and left hurriedly. And it was only when I was alone in my room that I allowed myself to cry.

Suddenly I heard a soft knocking on the door frame. "Just a moment," I said, sitting up. I wiped my eyes carefully. "All right."

The door swung in and Da crawled through. He kicked the door shut with his boot and sat down in a chair. In his hand he held a small lady's needler. It had belonged to the Lady Daedre, and he wore it into combat and on the hunt in its wrist holster, having punched new holes into the strap for his larger wrist. "I've always been meaning to give this to you when you grew up. Only I didn't realize that you already had, or nearly anyway." He smiled apologetically.

I touched the Earthstuff about my neck. "I already have my mother's pendant," I said.

"Well, I think you should have this too. It will keep the men in line even if your title doesn't."

I got up from my bed and knelt beside his chair. I touched his arm lightly. "Do you miss her very much, Da?"

Da scowled at me. "You know too much, lass."

"You wouldn't always know that from some of the things you say."

But Da wouldn't let me distract him. He reached a hand up and tilted my head toward the ceiling so he could study it. "You grew up too fast in some ways. You had to be the lady of the doom before you could be a woman. Has the blackguard proposed yet?"

"Caven? He's off on his ranging trip. And anyway, why should he?" I tried to sound casual.

"I can tell from the way he looks at you." Da smiled and leaned his head back against the chair.

"He has a funny way of showing his love. He prefers to lark among the trees and animals rather than be with me.

76

I'd as soon love a man of straw. At least he'd stay put."

Da pursed his lips and shrugged. "Well, it's in the blood."

We rarely spoke of such things among the Folk, for it only increased certain bitter feelings. But Caven's people had been crew members of one of the ships we had forcibly commandeered at the start of the Long Flight. The ships' crews had no choice but to go with us after we had left the world of the Fair Folk—even if we could have let them go —because the Fair Folk held us all equally guilty. Most of the ships' crews had intermarried among the Folk, settling down, however reluctantly. Some resentment remained, breaking to the surface every now and then in angry words or a fight. And many of the rangers who explored our wilderness—like Caven—had at least one starship crew member as a parent.

Da sighed, looking puzzled. "I wish your mother was here to advise you. I've searched and searched my memories of her for something to say to you, but the only thing I can remember is the day I proposed to her. I hemmed and I hawed for nearly an hour."

"I can't see you hesitating about anything, Da."

"Well, I did. Your mother had to come right out and tell me, 'My Lord, I am a simple person and the fancy talk is not for me. All I ask is that you be honest with me and with yourself—but mostly with yourself.' So I thought for a moment, and out of honesty I admitted I was a coward and asked her to marry me. And she did."

"You didn't hesitate about the Lady Daedre."

"That was different. I'd known your mother since she was a little private in the Ninth. There was something incestuous about marrying her."

"But you did."

"And glad I am." Da kissed me. "Now this old man will go off to be alone with his memories."

He left the needler and holster on the chair.

77

five

I

"Well, well, well." The Anglic looked up from the large chunk of driftwood he was polishing and whittling. He got up, a cautious smile on his face. "A long time since I've seen you folks together." He strode down to meet us, holding out his hand for a handshake.

Da took it, studying the Anglic's face. He seemed to have aged ten years, even twenty these last few years. And perhaps his smile and handshake were just a little bit too eager.

"Haven't much in the way of hospitality to offer you. But if you'll wait a moment, I'll run down to Ewen Cai and get the latest batch from his still. He's always needing a toy or two for his children."

"We're not here socially," Da said.

The Anglic rested his right hand on his belt near his gun. "What are you here for, then?"

"What does Maeve do at night?" Da asked.

The blood drained from the Anglic's face as if he already knew the purpose of our visit. "Nothing," he insisted. "Nothing at all. Why do you have to keep pestering us this way?"

It was well that Da had made my stepbrothers leave their weapons behind. Mihangel and Cularen would have rushed forward then, but Athvel held them back. "Leave this to me," he said. He nodded to the Anglic. "We think she goes out at night with the Seademons."

"Bosh," said the Anglic.

Athvel unwound the bandage from around his head. "Do you think I've imagined this, Anglic? It was Maeve gave this to me down by the Devil's Eyes."

"Are you sure it was her? In the dark . . ." The Anglic stopped fumbling helplessly for some excuse.

"Call her out, if you please," Da said.

The Anglic looked as if he wanted to refuse, but old habits die hard. He was too used to obeying Da. He turned reluctantly toward his doom.

"Maeve, you come out here."

She crawled through the doorway hesitantly, and before she even straightened up, she had run to the Anglic's side, clinging to him. She appeared very small and vulnerable, and yet there was a wild air to her—a feeling that at any moment she might change shape before our eyes—as if it were only the faith of the Anglic that held her to the form of a human girl.

Athvel put his hand in his belt pouch and stepped closer. Maeve pressed her head against the Anglic's arm. "I believe this belongs to you, Maeve." Athvel held out the comb.

The Anglic gripped both of Maeve's arms and he glared down at her. "You said you'd lost it."

"She did, but at the same place where she gave me this little remembrance of her." Athvel waved the comb at her.

Maeve's eyes were drawn from the comb up Athvel's arm to his face and the scar there. She tried to break free of the Anglic, but he was holding on to her arms and for a minute he struggled with Maeve, who made small, hurt, whimpering sounds.

"Maeve!" His voice cut through Maeve's cries. She stood still and the Anglic let go of her. She turned as if hypnotized, her eyes fastening on the comb again. Slowly she reached out her hand and slipped it out of Athvel's hand.

"Well—" Da let out his breath in a sigh—"so you do know the Seademons."

"They are Maeve's friends," Maeve admitted reluctantly. "They bring things to Maeve and they show Maeve things."

"How did you know them?" Da demanded.

"They are friends of the Lugashkemi. They used to give each other things." That was more than we had ever been able to get out of Maeve before this.

"Why didn't you tell me you were seeing the Seademons?" The Anglic demanded in a hurt voice.

"All the Anglic wants to do at night is sleep. Maeve was bored."

"Lord," the Anglic said, "I can't tell you how ashamed I feel. But I promise you she'll never see the Seademons again."

"On the contrary," Da said. "I want Maeve to tell them that we also are their friends." Da's voice had taken on an unusually warm tone.

Maeve looked up in surprise. "You will let Maeve go on seeing them?"

The Anglic looked as if he wanted to protest, but Da was already answering: "Yes, of course."

There were only a few of us down on the beach that first night. We sat a little farther back than Maeve. The moonlit water rippled and shone calmly until suddenly a black arrow-like object appeared on the water. Maeve stood up expectantly and we all held our breath as the large, one-eyed Seademon let the surf carry it onto the sand. But when it saw us, it dug its tentacles into the beach, ready to shove itself off, back into the sea.

I'd never seen them before except in some tri-d's that Caven and other rangers had taken. The accompanying reports had described them as squid-like, for they had conic bodies averaging some two meters in length with twelve

80

tentacles measuring another two meters. Each tentacle had a mouth at the end with a terrible gripping power, and there were four primary tentacles with retractible talons running along their insides. The Seademons used their bodies like jets, discharging water through their anal passages.

But the tri-d's and the reports did nothing to capture the sleek power of the creatures. This one looked like the jeweled whip of a god—some awesome, jealous god. Its cone-shaped body looked like the gemmed handle of the whip and its tentacles like thongs that had been dusted with crushed rubies. Terrible and majestic, it seemed the undisputed lord of the seas. It swung its head about so that its one good eye could study us.

"Now, Maeve," Da said gently. "Try to tell it that we're its friends."

Maeve's hands went through a number of gestures and pantomimes and she seemed genuinely puzzled when the Seademon did nothing but stare at us with the same cold, implacable look.

"Try telling it we mean it no harm, then," Da said.

And Maeve did until after an hour she had grown tired and petulant.

"You haven't told it we wanted to trade," Da said.

"But Maeve *has*. Maeve *has*." She pounded the beach with her fist near where she sat.

The Seademon, tense at that gesture, whipped its arms about and hissed.

"For God's sake. Now it's mad," Athvel said.

Maeve lifted her head suddenly as if studying the waving of the tentacles. "It wants Maeve to go with it."

"I don't think that's such a good idea," the Anglic said lamely.

"Let her go, Da," Losgann said. "It hasn't done her any harm in the past."

"She might as well go." Da waved his hand disgustedly.

"Maybe the thing will be in a better mood tomorrow."

"Lord—" The Anglic began to protest, but stopped as the Seademon humped itself up, the area of its body just before the tentacles swelling and mottling angrily.

Maeve got into her suit happily, ignoring the miserable Anglic. Then she put on her helmet.

"You be back by dawn," the Anglic warned her.

She nodded and smiled, all of us knowing she would be back when she wanted. Maeve held out her arms eagerly for the Seademon's embrace. A tentacle wound itself about her waist almost lovingly and lifted her gently up in the air. Maeve spread her legs instinctively just before the Seademon set her upon its back. Then she lay flat, clasping her arms and legs tightly against its body almost as if she were making love to it.

The tentacles tensed like steel cables and the Seademon shoved itself off from the sand just as the tide swept in and lifted it up. Using its tentacles like poles, it turned itself about easily and we saw its sides hollow in and then it skimmed over the surface of the water like a stone, sliding lower and lower into the bay until there was only the pearl-like globe of Maeve's helmet knifing through the sea, and then even that was gone, leaving nothing but the moonlight dancing on the surface.

"Lord," the Anglic said finally, "if she's ever to be a part of the colony, this must stop. I'll have less control over her the more time she spends with them."

"Would she be happy as one more colonist, Anglic?" Da asked.

The Anglic fumbled in his belt pouch and took out a small, twisted piece of driftwood. "Lord, I'd hoped to teach her our ways gradually so she would fit in."

"What did you tell me about those little statues you carve from wood?" Da scratched at his chin. "Yes, that you don't have to carve the wood into a statue. The statue's already

82

there inside the wood and it tells your hands how to free it."

"Making a human being and making a statue are two different things, Lord."

Da stood up. The wind blew his cloak tightly against his body and the sand whipped away like little sprites. "Your tunic's a bit ragged. Best trade some of those statues for some more cloth."

"I meant to, Lord, before this. But today when I went about, nobody would trade. The story's gotten out, you see, and everyone thinks my carvings are witched."

"Why do you go on whittling, then?"

"It gives me something to do while I'm waiting." There was already a small pile of chips in the Anglic's lap.

"Bring some of them over. I've a fancy for some of your carvings."

"My carvings aren't for everybody," the Anglic said.

"It would give me great pleasure," Da said, but the Anglic kept his back turned to Da. Da sighed. "Will you come up and have a drink with us, then? It's a little cold for old men like us to be out here."

"No, I'll stay down here."

Losgann looked up at Da and me. "I'll keep him company if he doesn't mind."

"I can't stop you," the Anglic snapped. He kept his face turned toward the bay, the chips spilling over from his lap now onto the sand.

II

That went on for nearly four months while we tried to expand our relationship with the Seademons; and despite Maeve's assurances, we seemed no closer to reaching an understanding with them than when we first began.

Usually I slept late in the mornings and then, taking a

lunch with me, I went off in the afternoons to study what I could of our records on X-T contact. But almost all of that had really been left to the Fair Folk and their explorers rather than to us, whose real task was only to conquer and keep the peace afterward. And there were so many variables such as alien physiology and semiology to be taken into account. Still I thought I might be able to find some clues to help us communicate with the Seademons.

Usually I headed for my favorite place in a grove of trees that grew in the grassy hills east of the holding. It was a grove of special trees, found, so far as we knew, only in this one little dell in the hills where the water drained down and made it possible for more than grass to grow. The trunks of the trees were as thin as wands—my hand could span each of them—and they soared upward about ten meters, with leaves only at the last three meters. They bent with the wind, but their roots were so deep that few were ever blown over. The trunks themselves were jet black and the leaves a translucent red. The grove was like a castle of the Fair Folk with slender pillars of obsidian vaulting to a ceiling cut from one gigantic ruby. Blue-winged flutter-by's—tiny blue-skinned mammals that flew by, flapping the thin, tough skin connecting their six legs—scattered through the trees as they always did in the summer of the world.

For company I'd taken along my chirpy, Yeats. Suddenly he bounded from my shoulder and streaked toward the grove. I walked a little faster, knowing that the chirpy only became excited over one other person. I found Caven waiting for me—I'd shown him the place when I was a child. Yeats sat on his shoulder, nuzzling his cheek, while he rubbed one finger against the soft white fur of Yeats' belly. Caven's crossbow lay beside him. His hair, uncut and unshaved in months, grew out shaggy all over his head and his beard was unkempt and yet the eyes were the peaceful eyes of Caven.

I stopped and leaned my hand against a tree, unsure of

84

what to do or say after our angry parting, for Caven was a somber man, moody and as wild as the forests he loved. We stared at one another awkwardly for a moment and then he rose—slowly so as not to dislodge Yeats. "Lady." He bowed formally to me and I wished suddenly that I could be a little girl again who could tumble with him freely. But instead I nodded and set down my reader's cube and took his hand.

"Caven, it's been so long. . . ."

"Too long," my chirpy said.

Caven stroked his beard with his free hand. "I suppose it has been. Aye, but you're a fine sight for my eyes."

The Lady Daedre would have known how to put him at ease, but I had no such arts, being a plain-spoken person. "Thank you." I sat down. "Maeve—"

"You can tell me of that later," he said too quickly, sitting down beside me. He seemed to wish to avoid that particular subject since it might lead to a fight. But, after all, the disaster he had predicted had not yet happened. In the awkward silence Caven twisted his head to look at Yeats' belly. "You've gotten fat, my friend."

"Not fat," Yeats said indignantly, folding his middle paws over his round belly.

"I'm surprised that Ciaran can carry you on her shoulder."

Yeats nipped his ear. Caven let out a yelp and Yeats slid down from Caven, scampering over into my lap. I put my arm protectively around Yeats. And for a moment I felt as free as in the old days and I laughed and Caven laughed with me.

Impulsively I reached out a hand and tugged at his beard. "Tell me, do you sleep with that inside or outside the blanket?"

He caught my hand. "I put half of it out and half of it in." He grinned. "But that's more like my old Ciaran."

"I thought there was something wrong with the old

Ciaran since you stayed away so long."

Caven frowned. "You know we weren't to speak of that."

I sat up straight, smoothing out my kirtle. "I'll have no traitors about me."

"I was speaking more for Athvel than for myself," Caven said. "Ask him if you like."

"Are you ruled by him in all things, then?"

"He is the Lord's son, the true heir."

"Haven't you a mind of your own?"

He rubbed his forehead slowly. "Whether I am ruled by you or ruled by him in this matter of the Tearless One, there is no way that I can be my own person."

"What would you, then?"

"That they be sent into exile—hard as that may be, it is yet the kinder thing."

"Leave her and the Anglic to the Seademons?"

"Aye. Each to his own."

"Why didn't you speak your mind before this?"

He put his hand on one of the trees and drew it down, sighting along the straight lines of its trunk. "Being between you and your stepbrother, Lady, is a bit like having to choose between a fuzzy and a Seademon." The side of his mouth curled up sardonically.

"Poor Caven," I laughed. "If we torment you so, why don't you just stay away?"

He shrugged. "The both of you have your compensations."

"The both?" I arched my eyebrows. "I understand my brother's attractions for you, but what possible good can I do you?"

Caven looked away. "I never thought you'd turn coy."

I touched the back of his hand, stroking his fingers lightly. "What would you have me say, then?"

"What you would." He twisted round and seized my hand, trapping it between both his hands. "For instance, what would you say if I stayed?"

"I'd not find it disagreeable."

Then Caven moved closer. "And what would you say if I kissed you?"

I put my arms boldly round his neck. "Will you stay for long?" I asked him.

"Yes, if you wish."

"What say is it of mine? You said you wanted to be your own person."

"Don't play with me, Ciaran. I'm mad for you."

I put my hand to his chest, stopping him. "You'd say that to the first woman you met. No, make that the first female anything."

"It's only you that I've been wanting to see, Ciaran, all these months."

"You really came back for me?"

"Aye."

I drew my hand away so he could lower his mouth to mine.

Da gave his permission. He would not have dared to do otherwise. I told him point blank that I'd have Caven or no one. And more, that we were going to move out of the doom.

"Nonsense, there's plenty of room for you here."

"I want one husband, not two, and if I stay here, Da, you know you'll always be meddling in our affairs."

Da looked a bit huffy. "Why, I'd do no such thing."

I hugged him tightly. "Once a Lord, always a Lord. But I love you anyway. Only if you want grandchildren and soon, you'd best leave me do it my way."

"Humph. How sharper than a serpent's tooth," Da grumbled. I hugged him again and his sour expression changed to good-natured acceptance. "Well, all right. But you visit me every day, you understand?"

"I understand, Da."

There were many marriages that year, for it was a happy

time. The summer fields gave promise of a good harvest to come; but more than the idea of full bellies in winter was something less tangible. For once again, the Taran calendar more or less coincided with the worldly year—as if there were a marriage between our old and new worlds.

We built our first house of slate in the area of the holding where many of the other young couples decided to live. Caven and my brothers brought the dark slate down from the quarry to the east, large slabs tied to the back of stumpies. All our faces turned dirty quickly, glistening with sweat under the fine blue powder, as we hewed the large chunks into thinner slabs for the roof and the walls and even for a little picket fence to keep the neo-pigs out of the garden we would have one day.

There was no material for the framework of a doom, you see, even if I would have had one, but I would not. There was something about the cool, deep color of the slate that I liked, and I could work designs into the walls in my spare time and Caven, too, could carve some of the strange things he'd seen ranging.

And after Phoil blessed the house, we entered and held our first little fete, slunky—a squirrel-like creature with purple fur and three eyes—and skitters—small, twelve-legged lizards—with enough whiskey and brandy for everyone. (Da would have given us jars from his own cellars, but Caven preferred to promise his next winter's catch of furs instead.) And there was all the dancing, singing, eating, drinking, toasting, and boasting that any of the Folk could have wanted for their wedding.

Da and my family were the last to leave. Da adjusted the veil of lace—the lace was taken from one of the Lady Daedre's dresses. "Caven's a good man. I should know. I've trained him proper for you." He kissed me and went on to say goodbye to Caven, who was waiting impatiently at the door. I heard Da giving Caven some kind of warning.

"Well," Mihangel said gruffly, "there's not much meat to

you, so Caven will have a bony ride. But I expect you'll fatten up soon enough."

"Aye," said Cularen. Both of them kissed me before moving on to Caven to give him *their* warnings.

And there was my little frog, Losgann. He hugged me quickly. "You've been a nag and a pest; but despite all of that, I forgive you. So if he should so much as raise a hand to you, I shall come over and stamp him into the ground."

He pecked me lightly on the cheek and I tousled his hair with a laugh. "I'll do my own stamping, thank you."

"Aye—" Athvel threw his silver scalp lock over his shoulder—"that's what I was afraid of." He leaned close to whisper in my ear. "I'm sorry to be losing the peacemaker in the doom, but I'm glad of a place of refuge. Be happy, sister." And he kissed me and hurried on to Caven.

I turned away for a moment to hide my tears and it was then I heard Caven slam the door shut. He was leaning with his back against it, laughing.

"What was so funny about being alone together finally?" I asked.

He straightened, holding up his hands. "Easy, love. Easy. I was laughing at their advice."

I started to take the pins out of my veil. "Oh, and what did they say?"

Caven stepped up behind me and pushed my hands away so he could finish taking out the pins. I waited patiently. "From what they told me, love, I'm either to take the bastinado to you, lock myself inside a cage, or make my peace with the One, for I'll never make my peace with you."

"Did they, now?" I felt the hairs on the back of my neck begin to bristle. "And what will you do?" I turned around angrily.

"Why, I'll follow my own mind and yours too, for it's us living together and not them. Now turn about and let me undo those buttons."

III

I could not invite Maeve—we had made up after a fashion
—to any of the wedding preparations or to the wedding
itself. There was already a great deal of grumbling about
her secret meetings with the Seademons and some very
wild stories about what she and they did. So it was not until
after the wedding that I was able to visit them and receive
my bridal gift: a bolt of fine linen cloth that, from the looks
of the doom, had emptied a large part of their sea treasures.
In place of the treasures were many of the Anglic's now
worthless carvings.

"What happened to your things?" I asked.

"Traded them to Rector Phoil and Pheodir. They'll not
find the likes of them."

"Thank you, then," I said. I made a note to myself to sew
what things I could for them.

Maeve sat in obvious puzzlement. She half reached her
hand out to touch my face, but drew it back. "Why has
Ciaran wiped away the maiden mark?"

I held the cloth against my breasts and smiled. "I'm a
married woman now." I motioned to my long skirt that
hung almost to mid-calf. "And so I'm also allowed to wear
a woman's skirt."

"Does Maeve have to put the mark on her forehead every
day?"

"Yes," the Anglic said. "Just the same as I—to show I'm
unmarried."

"But Maeve and the Anglic live together just the same as
Caven and Ciaran."

"It's not the same thing, Maeve," I said. I meant it in a
kindly way and would have gone on to explain, but Maeve
was no longer the shy little girl I had known.

She twisted around to face me. "Ciaran does not know
everything," she said fiercely.

"Maeve," the Anglic warned her sternly, "that is no way to talk to the Lady of the Holding."

Maeve glanced resentfully at the Anglic and then back at me and then, her lips pressed together, looked ahead stonily at the wall. The Anglic and I tried to talk for a little bit more, forcing ourselves to sound happy, but both of us were relieved when I left.

Caven was all for burning the cloth when he found out who it was from, but he relented when I said I would use it to make clothes for them and not us. Only I never got a chance to, for Maeve had appeared that afternoon with a bare forehead, much to the scandal of the holding. And, muttering in Lugashkemi, she had gone about stepping on one woman's shadow, chasing her into her very house, and demanded a bolt of cloth, which the woman gladly gave her. Da paid her later for the cloth, of course, but it was obvious that the clever Maeve knew what effect she had on the superstitious fools among the Folk and was trading on it.

The next time she appeared in public, she not only still had a bare forehead but wore the long skirt of a married woman—clumsily stitched together as if she had done it herself and with a hem that draggled all around.

When I tried to hint to her that she might offend the holding by acting in this manner, she only laughed at me in a saucy way.

"I am a woman now. I have a right."

I tried to explain that maturity was a social status and not a biological one, so that it was not proper for her to appear as a married person—just as the unmarried Losgann or Athvel could not wear the clothing of a married man or go about without the bachelor's mark.

"Propriety?" Maeve shook her head. "What does that mean? It varies from clan to clan and from people to people. Maeve will not live her life by a lot of silly rules."

I saw then that the Anglic had been continuing her edu-

91

cation with some of his own heretical notions that had gotten him a few reprimands in the past from the rectors. But when I spoke with the Anglic privately, he simply held up his hands. "Ever since she's been going out openly with the Seademons every night, I can't do anything with her."

And yet, for all of Maeve's independent talk, I saw how badly the poor thing sought security still. Even though she now seemed sixteen in true years, she would still sit in the Anglic's lap outside their doom and insist on being held and stroked. And she would kiss him often in a very warm fashion.

The Anglic tried his best. He traded away his precious dart gun for some fine, thin silk in hopes of bribing her to behave herself. And it worked after a fashion, for she reappeared with the maiden mark and without the long skirts, but instead she now wore kirtles and tunics of silk with nothing underneath so that one could see her body shimmering through the material. And the men took to watching her with sick, hungry eyes, for she was small and dark and beautiful. She also let her hair grow longer and fuller than ever before, giving her a wild, passionate, yet childish look.

But what really attracted the men's looks was the forbidden and knowing way she smiled and looked back at them —the way, it's said, that a houri of the Fair Folk looks at someone. She began appearing with little gold trinkets and bits of jewelry—like the silk, the loot from a dozen alien worlds—and everyone knew the Anglic had not given them to her. When I asked her who had given her those things, she insisted with an insolent smile that they were things she had found. And the women began to take soil and spit into it and throw it between themselves and Maeve lest she blast their wombs, and she would only laugh and rattle off strings of Lugashkemi, convincing the women that they really were being cursed.

And one afternoon I heard the cries of *Whoo-ree! Whoo-*

ree! Rocks rattled against our slate fence and suddenly there was a frantic hammering at our door. I jerked it open and Maeve fell in, her skirt torn and her arms and legs cut and bruised. Outside was a crowd of some twenty angry women with stones upraised. I looked at the little garden we had planted. The stones had partly demolished it. The sight of my angry face, as well as the realization that they had damaged our garden, brought them to their senses. They dropped their stones and took to their heels.

I came back in to see Maeve trying to pull some of the material back over one breast and crying because it was torn.

"I'll give you some of my spare things," I offered.

"This was lovely, lovely, and so smooth, and those bald ladies tore it," Maeve said. "Maeve wishes she *were* a witch. Then Maeve could kill them all."

"I won't defend what they did, but we warned you they would do something like this," I said.

"Can Ciaran mend it? Maeve will pay."

She began to pull one of her rings off her fingers, a signet ring that she wore on her thumb with a stone as big as my eye. Even though I knew I should, I couldn't refuse her. "I'll see what I can do," I said. "You don't have to . . ."

Maeve saw the direction of my look. She raised her leg and pulled the anklet ring off. It had been carved from pink stone shot with blue. "Would Ciaran like this?"

"Maeve, where did you get that?"

Suddenly remembering, Maeve closed her fist over part of the anklet. "Maeve found it."

"I know where you got it from."

Maeve hurriedly slipped the anklet ring over her ankle. "Maeve has to go."

"You can't go out like that." I got a tunic and a kirtle and threw them to her. "Here, put these on."

I waited until she had left the lane before I ran out my-self. Losgann was where he usually was—at the exercise field, exercising his charm more than his body. He sat in the center of an admiring circle of friends, including his old friend Ardui and my little Eriu, who was developing into a quiet, pretty girl. All of them called out warm greetings to me. I returned their greetings with a smile and a nod and chatted with them for a bit before I motioned to Losgann to come away with me. Reluctantly he pushed himself up from the turf and followed me. I turned, for the sake of his face before the others, and pretended to smile, though my words were angry ones. "How could you give away Mother's anklet?"

Losgann tried to charm me with his smile. "When we married you off, we thought we'd be rid of your scolding, Ciaran."

"That anklet was supposed to be your remembrance of Mother."

"It was only an old bit of jewelry, and it was mine to keep or mine to give away." Losgann tried to walk back to the others, but I grabbed his arm.

I spoke in a low, urgent tone to him. "Losgann, you must stay away from Maeve. Have you forgotten how she scarred Athvel?"

"She was only defending herself." Losgann shrugged free of my hand. "She had no way of knowing what was in Athvel's mind."

I studied his face. He still wasn't capable of hiding the truth from me. "You've been talking to her. Even meeting her on the sly."

"Well, what if I have?" He tossed his long, fair hair, which really needed a proper cutting, out of his eyes. "She's the only one who knows the Seademons well."

"Trading the anklet away for information?" I asked skeptically.

"All right. All right, old woman." Losgann held out his hands to me in appeal. "She's lonely and unhappy. Can you understand that?"

"With all those rings? She must have many other admirers."

Losgann pressed his lips tightly together for a moment. "Yes, she does. But they mean nothing to her. I gave her the anklet because I've so little of my own that's precious. Truly precious."

I had been caught up so much in my new life that I really hadn't noticed how much Losgann had grown up. I stroked his cheek. "You mustn't give your heart to Maeve. She'll only hurt you."

Losgann pulled away from my touch sullenly. "You're only saying that because you want to keep on using her for your own purposes. All her life people have been using her, manipulating her, ordering her about. At least *I* treat her like a person."

"What do you mean by that?"

"Nothing," he said stubbornly. "I've gone too far already."

"Just what has she been telling you?"

"It was told to me in confidence," he insisted stubbornly.

"Are you putting your personal sense of honor before the good of the Folk?"

"This is of no harm to the Folk."

"Let me be the judge of that."

"No, Ciaran. Can't you understand? I'm my own person too. I've my own life to lead, my own judgments to make, and if I make mistakes, well, I'll be the one to live with them." He stroked his mustache for a moment in an unconscious imitation of Da. I could have yanked out each whisker for the conceit it gave him.

"It won't end here," I warned him.

"I didn't think it would." He smiled and returned to his friends.

Da was of the same mind when I went to see him. But it wouldn't do simply to order the two of them to stop seeing each other. Losgann was too much of a Devlin for that to work. Something more alluring had to be found before Losgann could be drawn away from Maeve. Though Da disliked taking advantage of his lordship when it came to breaking the customs of the Folk, Da suddenly gave in to one of Losgann's requests, letting him join a group of eighteen-year-old recruits—Ardui among them—though Losgann was still half a true year too young. This way he might accept a year-long separation from Maeve, for he would have to go to boot camp and then to some distant posting.

It was a happy time that last evening when the young men and women tramped up the street, fresh from their initiation into the regiment, laughing and singing. The new initiates' heads gleamed where their hair had been shaved except for the small scalp lock. Losgann looked so fine in his uniform that I had to kiss and hug him and rub his head to reassure myself that he was still my Losgann. We called it a uniform, though it was made of our rough homespun, dyed green. I'd spent several nights and days embroidering the regimental insignia of the Ninth onto it: the Eagle, the Lion, and the Dragon holding up the nine circles. Done in so short a time, of course, it wasn't anything but a crude one. Even so, Losgann did not care. As we sat in the great hall, Losgann would finger his patch every now and then as if hardly believing he had come of age. By the lamplight he looked much older—a stranger.

We ate and drank and toasted, and when I left the table to get some air because it was stuffy inside the hall, I heard someone follow me out through the extra-large tunnels leading through the outer rings of dooms forming Doom Devlin.

"A lovely night," I heard Losgann say when we were outside.

"Yes." Distantly I heard a group of the Folk singing one

of the old songs in celebration. "It's so rare when we can all enjoy such a night."

"You know, it won't work, Ciaran." Losgann leaned his back against the side of one of the dooms. "I know all this was your doing. No, don't try to deny it. You never used the stick on me when you could use a bit of candy to make me go where you wanted." He folded his arms and crossed one leg over the other. "Oh, don't worry. I'm going away, but I'm doing it because I want to show you something. I won't see Maeve for an entire true year, but when I come back, she'll be waiting for me though we've been apart all that time."

"Is that what she said to you?"

Losgann shrugged. "I can see it in her eyes." Suddenly he sprang straight up and kissed me lightly. "For once in your life, Ciaran, someone is going to tell you *no.*"

I studied Losgann with approval. Before this, he had had all the trappings and shape of a man, but now he was beginning to be one inside. I thought again of how Eriu had looked at him with such shining eyes. She would be more than willing and so would Losgann, for I was sure that he would outgrow this passion for Maeve despite all his fine words to the contrary.

And then Da poked his head through the door and called for us to come back in. They needed two more voices to do justice to "O, the Seas of Antares."

I followed Losgann back into the doom, my head full of plans for Eriu and Losgann.

Poor Losgann. I never had a chance to try to match him with little Eriu, for he was dead within the year.

IV

Though Maeve and I never discussed Losgann, Maeve became unco-operative after he left. After only a minute's try at communicating with the Seademon, she would insist that the Seademon did not want to talk and instead she would go off for one of her long sea rides, leaving the Anglic to brood more and more as he kept his lonely vigil on the beach. I would have thought more about it, but I became distracted by other things. I found that I was pregnant—something which almost caused Caven and Da and my step-brothers to come to blows as they tried to decide what to name the child.

It was near the end of the true Taran year and toward the end of Fancyfree's autumn when the great storm clouds rise up from the sea, great, hulking black monsters that charge over the dead, empty land, and the sea itself becomes a dullish milky brown. Caven was working on a hardwood cradle while I and some of the younger Folk of our lane tried to fashion some baby clothes when we heard the hullabaloo from the south end of the holding. The cries and voices grew louder as they came up our lane and I heard the snorting of a stumpy humping its way up the street. I stepped out of our house and saw Ardui, a fellow boot and Losgann's friend, guiding the stumpy along through the crowd. Behind him, across the back of the stumpy lay something in canvas. The men and women of the crowd clamored at him to tell them who the person was, but Ardui kept his peace.

My hands tightened for a moment on the slate pickets of our fence, telling myself that the bundle could not be for us. It would not stop at my house but at some other person's house. But Ardui halted his stumpy by our gate.

Ardui looked down at me. "I'm sorry, Lady."

I opened the gate and went to the stumpy and reached up almost on tiptoe. I could just touch the canvas shape of my poor little frog. "How did it happen?"

"Best I say it to your whole family, but I wanted to be sure you were there, so I've come here first. Sometimes the bearer of bad news suffers for the message and burden he carries."

We gathered in Da's room with Mihangel sitting near the door so he could check to see if there were any eavesdroppers in the tunnel.

Da stood with his hands clasped behind his back, his legs spread, and looking down balefully at Ardui. "Out with it, lad."

"Wait," I said, and got some whiskey for the pale Ardui. He gulped it down in one swallow and the blood rushed to his cheeks.

"Officially," Ardui said, "he slipped and fell on the rocks."

"Losgann was as sure-footed as a goat," I said.

"And so what is it unofficially?" Athvel asked.

Ardui twisted one of his wrists, looking around at us nervously. "He told me everything before he left that night. Fool that I was, I should have reported it to the Lieutenant, but Losgann talked about it so easily that I thought he was only going for a walk to write some of that poetry of his." And he told his story then in fits and snatches, needing fortification from the whiskey jar when a glower or growl from Da or one of my stepbrothers put Ardui in fear for his life.

I had given no thought to the fact that the rookery lay in that direction, near the battery where our Losgann stood his lonely watches. I can see it now, the lonely young man, really only a boy, standing on the concrete parapet by the old missile-launchers under their protective sheets of plastic: like huge beetled insects in translucent cocoons. Or eggs waiting to hatch some deadly insects.

And in the twilight—in that special time of the One even before dreams seem to stir—the light hangs soft on the hills and the sea is a deep, deep black. You can see every fish as it rises to the top, for it leaves a fiery wake of phosphorescent plankton. And there are little green lines etched across the surface of the sea like a picture, only the picture and the pattern of lines are always changing. And from far away the sound of the ocean surge drifts up the rocks.

It was then that he saw a fiery shape on the beach, covered all over with planktonic animals so that it glowed like a ghost. Our little frog was a brave lad, more's the pity. Before he called out the watch, he decided to have a closer look. He climbed down the rocks and, in so doing, momentarily lost sight of the figure. By the time he got down to the base of the cliff, the creature had had time to shed its suit. He saw it was Maeve, the Tearless One, naked now, kicking at the surf that surged up about her ankles so the spray flew out in fiery waves. It must have been the first time she had come here or she would have been reported before.

Losgann stepped out from behind the rocks. "What are you doing here?"

"Maeve thought Little Frog might be lonely, but if Little Frog is busy . . ." The Tearless One started to turn away.

Losgann held out his hand. "No, please don't go." With a smile she put her hand in his. "It's so marvelous having you here, but how did you ever get to this place? Did the Seademons bring you?"

The Tearless One frowned. "Now Little Frog sounds like the others. All the time they ask questions."

"Yes, I know." Losgann took his hand away and uncocked his crossbow. "I'm sorry."

The Tearless One stood with that disconcerting nonchalance she had about nudity. The only thing she wore was the anklet ring he had given her. "No more questions?" she asked.

"No more questions," Losgann said. They spent most of Losgann's watch talking about various things, relaxing with one another in a way they had never been able to do back in the holding with everyone about. And Maeve promised to be on the beach at the same time tomorrow, and with a heady feeling of rebellion Losgann promised not to tell anyone that he had seen the Tearless One.

And through the nights they drew closer to one another, moving to that final moment they knew would come, but Losgann was surprised when the Tearless One appeared on the beach in her long marriage dress and wearing a bride's floral wreath—both of which she must have brought in a waterproof bundle. And she led him to a sandy hollow at the base of the cliffs, hidden by the rocks.

They met every night there by the sea. And on their last night together, before Losgann was to be rotated to an inland holding, he asked the Tearless One to marry him.

"But Maeve and Losgann are already married. The sea is the witness."

"No, I mean a ceremony before the Folk so we can live together."

"Maeve cannot live with Little Frog." The Tearless One seemed troubled.

"Why not?"

"Maeve is married to the sea," the Tearless One insisted. And when Losgann pressed her for an explanation, she told him; for the Tearless One could be as changeable in mood as the sea, by turns loving and then angry and spiteful. What she told Losgann, Ardui did not know, for Losgann said it was too shameful to repeat.

But after she had spoken to Losgann, the Tearless One tried to touch him, but he pushed her away. Sadly the Tearless One stripped off her clothes and climbed back into her suit and swam away to the tentacles of her one-eyed Seademon.

Losgann must have walked back up to his station and brooded about it all night. And Ardui, worried about him since he was so pale and wan the next day, questioned him. And finally Losgann told him and then left. Ardui thought about telling the Lieutenant right then, but decided it would be better if Losgann reported the matter after his walk. Only he never returned. They found his body among the rocks below the parapet.

Athvel, lounging on Da's bed, suddenly sat up and asked skeptically: "Losgann told you all this?"

"Yes, Lord, yes," Ardui insisted.

"Da," Mihangel said suddenly, "there's a commotion in the holding."

One by one, we crawled out into the tunnel and onto the holding, where we stood by the doorway. All the others already there turned to look at us. Maeve, the Tearless One, stood beside the canvas-shrouded Losgann on the table. She was wearing her married woman's long dress and the bride's floral wreath about her neck, and in her great sorrow was grunting loudly and so fast that she lost her breath, but no tears fell.

"Get her away," Da said. His voice was as quiet and deadly as a knife slipping out of its sheath. "Get her out of this doom."

It took four men to hold her away from Losgann. Though she was small, she was wiry. And she looked like some demoness with her hair all tangled and her eyes wild, and she slipped into her inhuman Lugashkemi to curse us all as the men dragged her from the doom.

Everyone waited for Da's next word, but all he said was, "Tell the Anglic that neither he nor his foster child is welcome at the wake." Stooping, he re-entered his tunnel. One by one, my stepbrothers followed him.

I kept an eye on them all through the wake, and when they slipped away, I followed them to Da's room. They were drinking quietly from one of the red jars of whiskey and looking somber. Tucked away in Da's belt I saw his broad-bladed knife. It was made long ago by some warlock-smith who forged the blue steel and carved the handle. It had been won by Da when he had first begun fighting for the Fair Folk, wresting it from a priest's hand within a temple. He said it was a sacrificial knife, but I had never seen him wear it till now.

Looking about the room, I felt as if I were not inside our doom but had somehow entered a cave of Stone Age savages. I was not facing my family: not my wise, mighty da, nor the learned Athvel, nor Mihangel, clever with his hands, nor Cularen, who summoned giant golden wheat out of the stoniest ground. It was as if they had shed their masks to reveal the true savages they were. "What are you going to do?" I asked.

"We must end the Lady's Curse now." Mihangel looked to Cularen, who nodded. For once, Da and my stepbrothers were all in agreement, though Athvel felt it necessary to put it in his own words.

"It's through my folly Losgann has met his death. If I hadn't been so weak and given in to the Anglic that first night or asked Da to spare her life, we'd still have our little frog with us."

"If anyone's to blame, it's me," I said, aware of all their angry, hostile eyes turned toward me. "If I hadn't meddled, their romance might have just faded away. I think they got together as much because they resented my trying to separate them as because they liked one another." Each member of my family looked at me now as if I had changed into a creature as strange as Maeve. "Try to think of what she meant to Losgann."

Athvel slipped his Earthstuff—the dagger of metal said to come from the hull of the very first ship to carry our ancestors into the stars—from its belt sheath. As if in reproach of me, Mihangel handed him a whetstone and with equal solemnity he accepted it and began to sharpen the dagger with a slow, rasping sound. "Aye, I've in mind what she meant to Losgann: it destroyed him in the end."

"What about our duty to the Folk? Trying to kill her might make the Seademons angry and they'd take it out on our people."

Da lowered the jar of whiskey and wiped his mouth with the back of his hand. "The Hounds of Ard-Ri were never afraid of trouble. We've offered them the hand of friendship and those creatures could not or would not understand. In all this time that we've tried to communicate with them through the Tearless One, we've become no friendlier."

The room stank with their liquored courage and their fear, for they were all of them sweating. Their breathing was coming quick and short from their excitement, almost in counterpoint to the rhythmical rasp-rasp-rasp of Athvel's dagger on the whetstone. It was a savage time.

"I'll have none of this." I started to turn away, feeling both lonely and angry. "The Anglic must know."

Athvel blocked my way. "You'll tell him nothing, Ciaran." He raised the point of his dagger menacingly. "Or I swear I'll cut your throat myself."

I tilted back my head to expose my throat. "Then do it, Athvel. Do it now."

I watched as the anger and fear gave way to agony in Athvel's eyes. He threw the whetstone away so that it rattled against a pane, and with the hand that had been freed he rubbed his forehead. "I don't know what came over me, Ciaran. Forgive me."

"It's a terrible thing," Da observed, reaching for an unopened jar of whiskey, "when a sister does nothing to avenge her brother's death."

"Can't you understand?" I shook my head in frustration. "The Tearless One is not of the Folk. She never willingly accepted our ways."

Da considered that as he broke the seal on the new jar. Being fair with people was almost a habit by now after all these years of leading the Folk. I also think he was a bit surprised by my stubborn resistance. It made him check his anger a bit—partly because he did not want to see his family become further divided. "You're truly set in your mind, then?"

"I am."

"Then speak to them. I'll give you no more than half an hour and then we'll be coming. Mind you," he added as he raised the jar to his lips, "you're not to be there."

"Aye, I won't be there." I could give him that much.

I ran through Doom Devlin, past the wake and up the streets, ignoring the people who called to me. Then I was running through the fields the short distance to the hills and up the path. The Anglic was outside whittling, with the Tearless One sitting at his feet, watching him as she often did. Her marriage dress was torn and her floral wreath, broken when she had been thrown out of Doom Devlin, hung forlornly about her neck.

"Ciaran," the Tearless One said hopefully.

I ignored her and faced the Anglic instead. "You must leave," I told him.

The Anglic's knife poised over the wooden block in his hand. "I never ran from a fight in my life. No one can tell me to leave."

"Then I'm asking you."

The Tearless One had taken my arm. "Ciaran, what is wrong?"

But I pulled free. "You know about Losgann, then?" I asked the Anglic.

"Caven told me," the Anglic said. He settled his back against one of the metal frames of his doom. The Tearless One kept on pulling at my arm.

"They'll kill you if they find you here," I said.

"I'll kill one or two of them before that happens."

"Yes, and I'll have to mourn for more people. Do you know just what you are protecting? You've probably only heard rumors and half-truths. Now listen to everything."

105

And I told him what I knew of Losgann. "Now ask her what she's done that drove poor Losgann to his death."

The Tearless One had stopped trying to get my attention during the story. The Anglic looked at her now. "Do you want to tell me?"

The Tearless One shook her head.

The Anglic studied the block of wood for a moment and then threw it far away down the hill. He slipped his knife into the sheath. "We'll leave," he told me.

"Ciaran!" The Tearless One's voice grew insistent for attention now. But she drew back when I turned so she could see my face.

"I never want to see you again," I said. Then I walked away.

"Ciaran?" The Tearless One called out, but the Anglic must have stopped her.

"We've got a lot of packing to do, child, and quick too."

six

I

Da and my stepbrothers smashed every one of the heavy panes of glass, though it took several hours. They worked slowly and methodically until the frames were completely empty. Then they allowed the Folk to loot—greed being a stronger emotion than fear. Da and my stepbrothers were not vicious men and, no matter what they said, the destruction of the Anglic's doom and its treasures would be enough to sicken them, for it's never an easy thing to see how ugly you can be. They filed by me silently, ashamed to look at either me or Caven when we arrived later. We listened to the howling and roaring laughter of the Folk pillaging what little the Anglic had left.

Everyone instantly grew quiet, though, when we heard the shots. "That's from the bay," Da said.

It was amazing the effect that the shots had upon the mob, for they changed from howling beasts fighting over the spoils back into the disciplined soldiers they were. Da shouted to various men and women to fetch arms and call out the rest of the watch. Then he and my stepbrothers and I ran down through the lanes past the cottages and then the dooms with the mob close at our heels, snatching up weapons as we ran, from rakes and hoes to rocks. And sometimes I'd see someone dash ahead and call everyone out of a cottage or doom with whatever they had inside, whether it was crossbows or kitchen knives.

We found the Tearless One bending over the bloody corpse of the Anglic, and the large, one-eyed Seademon was lying on the beach behind them, swinging its bloodied tentacles over its head and hissing. The Tearless One stood up uncertainly. Her suit was covered with the Anglic's blood. For someone who did not know her, her grunting sorrow made her sound almost like an animal. "Witch!" Cularen shouted. He threw a rock at her. "Witch!" Others took up the cry. Cularen's rock landed in the sand near her feet.

She hesitated, looking toward the Seademon. It hissed to her, gesturing impatiently with its tentacles, and drew its long body farther up onto the sand. Running, she picked up her helmet and leaped upon its back. Crossbow darts kicked up the sand—Mihangel had found the watch's crossbows by then—but the Seademon was already twisting around and plunging into the sea, its body trailing behind it.

"Get to the boats," Da shouted.

And while the others streamed away to obey Da, I knelt beside the Anglic.

"It's already too late," Caven said. "She'll be long gone before they've even got the motors started."

"I don't know whether I hope she gets away or not," I said. The Anglic had one arm flung out, revealing a wrist gun like the one Da had given me. The other hand had been fumbling at the neck of his suit as if he had been trying to get his helmet off. I pushed his hand away and worked at the seals. Caven lifted him partly from the sand while I eased off his helmet. The blood had begun to dry around his mouth and nose; and his eyes were wide open. I closed them for him while Caven took off his own shirt and dipped it into the seawater so we could wash off the Anglic's face.

I started to fold his arms across his stomach, but when I picked up his helmet to set it up by his head, a shiny silver disk fell out. It was a recording tape disk of the kind—the size of a nail—that rangers used while exploring. The disk could be attached inside the helmet near the mouth and was activated at the word *start*. I gave no more thought to it at that time, pocketing it and then going to find some rectors to fetch the corpse for burial. It was only later when Caven and I finally were back in our cottage and undressing for bed that I put my hand inside my tunic pocket ,and found the disk. Curious, I sat down on our bed and told the disk to rewind, hearing the high, thin whining sound as it did so. When it was ready, I told it to play back. And from the disk, in a ghostly whisper, the Anglic's voice began to rise. Caven sat up and I held it between us so we could both lean close to hear his rambling, disjointed account of his years with the Tearless One.

II

As the Anglic said, it was as if he had never been fully alive until Maeve came into his life. She took such pleasure in the simplest things. She was delighted with his doom, dancing about and trying to catch the colored pillars of light. He tried to get her to sleep on her own pallet that first night, but wound up having to take her under his blankets again, her head next to his heart.

Maeve tagged after him all the next day as if she were afraid of losing him; and he felt complimented, never having had or wanted anyone to depend upon him before this. He had some of my old kirtles and he traded some of his souvenirs and other things for more tunics and kirtles for her. And he taught her to comb her hair, to bathe, and in general loved her as the family he had never had—which surprised him because he had never thought of himself as enjoying this sort of thing.

And though Maeve came to talk fairly well, her language and her manners were only tolerable—even by the rough

109

standards of the Folk—and the Anglic knew that this was nothing more than a thin shell over the strange, wild, tempestuous creature she really was. At first he had hoped that going to the rectory would help her to adjust, but after the trouble with Radog the Anglic knew he would have to try to "humanize" her—as he called it—by himself.

For their own sake, the Anglic took Maeve more and more into the wild. They wandered through the forests and the mountains far to the east or along the northern seas. He showed her everything that was strange and wonderful and beautiful about Fancyfree in the hope that she would come to love her new world. He showed her the star trees, and the paradise birds with wings like rainbows and voices like angels, and the giant spider webs that the winds sang through. Hunters would cross their path occasionally and bring back reports that both the Anglic and his creature looked well.

But then she became indifferent to her studies after their novelty had worn off. It was clear that she missed the sea, and it said something about the bond between her and the Anglic that, though she was forever in sight of the sea, she never once went down to the shore. And yet the Anglic could see how wistful Maeve grew when she looked out at the sea and how eagerly she studied anything which dealt with the sea. He had avoided taking her down, thinking it better to break all ties with her past, but he now thought himself wrong. It would be better to wean her away gradually.

The problem, as the Anglic now figured it, was that Maeve still lived too much in her past. This world did not seem like home to her. "Come along," he finally said. "Get everything packed."

"Are Maeve and the Anglic going to the mountains?"

"No, to the sea. Just to study," the Anglic warned her. "And if you don't learn better, then it's back up here we go."

"Oh, Maeve will study. She will." Because it would take so long to dry, Maeve even suffered letting her hair be cut —though not as short as some child of the Folk, for she insisted that her hair must at least reach her shoulders.

That next day they got his stumpy from the pen and rode south for a bit before turning west, for the Anglic knew of a private little beach there.

Maeve could barely conceal her excitement as they neared the sea. As soon as she got within sight of the beach, she slid down the stumpy's side and ran helter-skelter down the path. The Anglic had an anxious ten minutes while she swam about with ease and grace surpassed only by the Seademons; but though she complained when the Anglic called her, she came back. The Anglic set her to her lessons then with a microfilm on basic botany. She studied better by the sea, apparently having more confidence in herself. But then she tried to curl up on the Anglic's lap, making her body plastic against his as if she had no bones at all.

"It's too hot to study this way," the Anglic said.

"There is no one to see Maeve and the Anglic. Not like back among *them.*" She picked up his hands and moved them down along her arms.

"We shouldn't do this, Maeve. You're too old."

"The Anglic does not love Maeve?"

"Yes, yes . . . ," the Anglic sighed. He began to stroke her arms lightly, hoping that no one would see them and misunderstand, for the Lugashkemi had liked to touch one another warmly and Maeve was used to being held and rocked and touched, so that she often demanded such displays of affection at night. To her, the one compensation for living on the land was that she could actually feel someone's touch; before this, the Lugashkemi had usually had to touch her through her suit unless they landed on some world with the right atmosphere for Maeve.

But then there came one day when the Anglic lay drowsing by the sea. Raising his eyelids finally, he saw Maeve standing waist deep in the water. His mind was on other things when he noticed Maeve staring, apparently fascinated by her reflection on the sea surface. But then the wind shifted and came from the sea. The stumpy got up on his six legs and stomped about restlessly. The Anglic got up and called Maeve to him. Reluctantly, Maeve turned away, but the Anglic thought he saw the water ripple as if large air bubbles rose from beneath.

During the next trip to the beach the Anglic had a feeling that something waited now in the sea, just out of sight, waiting for him to relax one moment in watching Maeve. But the Anglic did not. It was on the trip after that that Maeve showed more cunning than the Anglic had thought she had. She took him for a vigorous swim before lunch. The exercise, combined with lunch and the warm air, soon made him drowsy. Maeve suggested that they both take a nap. She lay down beside him and put her arms about him and soon they both fell asleep, or so he thought. When he woke up, Maeve was again in the sea, standing waist deep, whispering. He quietly walked down to the beach.

Maeve's reflection floated over the surface, and at his angle of vision it was hard to see into the water; but it seemed that there, flickering beneath Maeve's reflection, he saw an eye, one large red eye where her breasts should have been reflected. Maeve turned around startled and he thought he saw a red shape swirl about, but he could not be sure. Maeve slipped and fell into the water as if a sudden tug of the surf had pulled her down; but he was convinced that the water had begun to ripple a moment before and that Maeve had only been masking the creature's exit.

Maeve came up spluttering. He pulled her onto the beach. "Who were you talking to, Maeve? The Lugashkemi?"

"No," Maeve said, "Maeve swears that there are no Lugashkemi here."

"Was it a Seademon?"

"The Anglic said himself that he didn't think the Seademons were very intelligent."

In frustration, he grabbed her shoulders and shook her. "Don't you lie to me."

"Maeve isn't lying," Maeve said, frightened.

"Or tell half-truths."

"Maeve isn't," she insisted.

He touched her wet locks. "Well, it's best to be going home now." He added, "But we'll come here no more." He was curious to see how Maeve would react.

"But—" Maeve began.

"No arguments," he said sternly.

On the way home he thought no more about it, not daring to.

But Maeve's very happiness depended upon the Anglic's mood, and his angry silence confused her so that she needed more reassurance. That night she crept into his pallet to be held, and because of what had happened that afternoon he did not chase her out after a few minutes as he usually did. And he began to soothe her. But at what we thought were ten true years Maeve was a child and yet not a child. And he began to touch her, but not as a child.

And the next day the Anglic could not look at her because of his guilt and shame, but Maeve misinterpreted it as anger with her and so that next night she again sought reassurance. When the Anglic tried to make her leave his pallet, she began the hysterical grunting sounds that she called crying. Her tear ducts were normal enough, but somehow she was never able to equate sadness with an overflow of her tear ducts. She would simply sit as she did right then with her face screwed up in misery, her body breathing heavily, even convulsively. After ten minutes of this, the Anglic held out his arm and she curled up against his side. He meant only to stroke her back, but his hand crept downward to her buttocks, then to her hip, then her thigh. . . .

113

So their new relationship began and Maeve could never understand the Anglic's shame and guilt the next morning. And once he held her tightly against him while he soiled her legs and she clapped her hands against her sides to show her approval, but the Anglic would only sit embarrassed. She had often, it seemed, watched the Lugashkemi mate and had even been allowed to help in the long, complicated, quadri-sexual process.

Even if the Anglic had wanted to, there was no real way of stopping her. And when they were finished, he would always fall into a deep, heavy sleep from which he awakened only at dawn. The years seemed to pass by quickly until Maeve was fifteen. Then came that strange day when they tried to give me my welcome-home present after my boot year and we all made those crazy accusations.

Afterward, he sat with the sad Maeve. When she was sad and silent, she seemed especially like a child. "It's just a little spat." The Anglic tried to encourage her. "Ciaran'll come around and apologize."

"She said I was never to do that," Maeve said, puzzled.

"Do what?" the Anglic asked, beginning to feel afraid.

"Do this." And Maeve leaned forward and kissed the Anglic as he had taught her. And she reached her hand between his thighs.

"You touched Ciaran there?"

"She wanted to know what Maeve did at night."

"And you told her?"

"Maeve was starting to show her. And then she got mad."

The Anglic slumped forward, letting his forehead rest in his hands. She brushed his leg lightly. He pushed her hand away. "No, we mustn't ever do that again. We must be strong."

"But what is wrong about it?"

"We mustn't ever," he repeated, more for himself than for Maeve.

114

"As the Anglic wishes," Maeve said, sad and perplexed. To her it was only warm friendship to perform this natural act together. And no matter how the Anglic tried to din morality into her, it never seemed to register. And she came no more to his pallet, so that the Anglic was left to his troubled sleep.

And one midnight he heard Maeve stir on her pallet and pad lightly across the floor. She kissed him lightly on the cheek before she left the doom.

He got up after she had left. Her nightdress lay on the floor and her diving suit and gear were gone—the outfit had been a special present to Maeve. He pulled on his clothes and hurried after her, following her in the double moonlight through the holding to the beach. She crouched by the last of the cottages at the edge of the beach and waited till the watch had marched past, patrolling the long distance around the bay. Then she sprinted out to the rocks before she put on her suit, flippers, and breather pack.

He heard her call something low and guttural to the waves and she rocked back and forth on her rock as eagerly as some girl waiting for her lover—waiting as if she had done this many times before. Tentacles rose from the sea, groping their way over the rocks with small, hissing, slithering sounds until they touched Maeve's knee. They caressed her leg momentarily and she held her arms cooperatively above her head while a tentacle coiled itself about her waist. Then, quickly before the watch could see, it lifted her carefully from the rock where she sat. When she had put on her helmet, it drew her under the sea. And there was no more than a strange set of ripples flickering over the surface as the Seademon carried her away into the night.

The Anglic felt jealous and hurt and frightened, all at the same time. He paced back and forth until, when it was almost dawn, Maeve came into the doom. She got a rag and began to wipe the water from her suit, humming contentedly to herself. She had never noticed the Anglic sitting on the pallet.

"Where were you?" the Anglic asked harshly.

She stood up as if she had been lashed. "The Anglic was spying on Maeve!"

"And with good reason." The Anglic stood over Maeve. "Why did you fool me?"

"Fool the Anglic? Maeve never fooled the Anglic. If the Anglic had asked, Maeve would have told him."

"You're not to go near the Seademons again."

"But why, Anglic? They're Maeve's brothers. The Sea—"

"You have to stay with your own kind," the Anglic insisted stubbornly.

"Why?"

The Anglic pulled at his whiskers. What had mankind ever done for Maeve except to curse her? And yet Maeve could not go on leading this double life. "I'm human, Maeve. Don't you love me?"

Maeve held him tightly. "But Maeve *does*. Doesn't Maeve do everything the Anglic says when he is awake?"

He stroked her hair quietly. "You do, child. You do."

"Can't the Anglic share Maeve?"

It would have been so easy to let things go on as they were. The Anglic would not live much longer, and Maeve could make him so happy. But he could not be selfish. There was Maeve's own future happiness.

"What will you do when I'm dead, Maeve?"

"The Anglic will never die."

"I will, someday," he said gently.

"Then Maeve dies too."

"No, you have to go on. Promise me." He took her head between both his hands and tilted it back so he could look at her eyes. She began to grunt sadly. "Promise me."

"Maeve promises," she said in a small voice.

"And promise me you'll live with our kind."

"The Anglic is Maeve's kind. The sea folk are Maeve's kind."

"No. No." The Anglic knelt down before her, holding on to her shoulders. "The Folk of the holding are your own kind."

"They make fun of Maeve; they even spit at Maeve."

"That doesn't matter. Their bodies are like your body. Their minds are like your mind."

"The Anglic is not like them; Maeve is not like them."

The Anglic knew now that he was paying the penalty of not fighting the prejudice in the holding and forcing the Folk to accept her. He had a great sense of failure and loss, and he cursed himself because he had been unable to protect the person whom he had loved the most. And yet he knew no answer, for it was clear that Maeve would not obey him and might even leave him for the Seademons. He would rather have her on any terms than lose her.

And so he said and did nothing until Athvel returned with his scar. And the Anglic was forced to sit by while the Seademons openly took her away each night. He tried to be patient, but finally he confronted her in private and asked her what she did with them.

Maeve was in one of her playful moods. "What does the Anglic care?" She shrugged her shoulders saucily. "He wants only to sleep at night."

"Do you have company besides them?" For she was wearing long dresses now and receiving presents she did not try to hide from him.

Maeve hesitated.

"Don't lie to me, child. Do you?"

"It's just that Maeve gets lonely and it is so dark. Maeve needs company."

"Is it the Seademons?"

"They are Maeve's friends."

"Who else is Maeve's friend?"

"You."

"And who else?"

"He made Maeve promise never to tell." And no amount of arguing or threats could force Maeve into telling his name.

It was Losgann, of course.

III

She had sat very still after I had warned them and gone away.

"Maeve must go away," Maeve said finally. "Maeve must go away by herself. Maeve only hurts those who try to help her."

"Might as well cut off this arm now, child," grumbled the Anglic. "I'll go with you."

"To the sea?"

"To the mountains," the Anglic snapped.

But Maeve was no longer a girl, but a woman. "Maeve must go to the sea."

And as the Anglic saw it, there was only one way to save her now. If she would not turn away from the Seademons, then he must make the Seademons turn against her—no matter how cruel and treacherous it might seem to Maeve at the time. "All right, to the sea, then," he agreed. "Will you take me with you tonight?" he asked.

"Oh, yes. Oh, yes." She held on to him excitedly and he managed only with difficulty to keep his resolve. They got their suits together and hastily assembled their bundles, having to leave behind the few precious things the Anglic had not traded away. The Anglic left the packing to Maeve and while she was distracted he went to one shadowed part of the doom to prepare, having taken an old souvenir from his war kit. They left soon after that for the beach, waiting among the rocks, where they put on their suits. While the two-man patrol was at the other end of the beach, they slipped into the sea. It was while they hid in the bay waters that the Anglic began telling his story into the tape disk, for he wanted someone among the Folk to know that the fault for what had happened was his, not Maeve's.

Maeve had told the Anglic that the Seademon would be coming at midnight and so just before that time he put his helmet against Maeve's and shouted to her he was having trouble with his breather pack and had to go ashore. As he expected, Maeve went with him.

The Anglic was taking a chance, of course, that my da and stepbrothers would not have figured out where he was hiding and be waiting there, but he needed to bring the Seademon at least partly out of the sea. So he rose out of the sea suddenly, catching the watch by surprise. He stunned them with narco darts from his crossbow and waded up onto the beach, where he began to tinker with his pack. We had to picture the rest from what we heard on the tape.

When it was time, Maeve called the low guttural name softly to the sea. With his back to the sea and Maeve, the Anglic slipped the little wrist gun over his arm, having taken it from his suit pocket. With a hard flick of his wrist, the Anglic cocked it and turned. If the Seademons thought that Maeve had lured one of them into a trap, they might avoid her, binding her irrevocably to human kind. Maeve was puzzled when no Seademon came. She called again. When still no Seademon rose, Maeve told the Anglic to step back. She did not turn her head around, though, to look at him.

Reluctantly, the Anglic withdrew farther up the beach. He was ready when the large, one-eyed Seademon rose out of the water. Maeve was in his way, so he had to shift position. He ran awkwardly because he had not taken the fins off his boots. Maeve turned around in astonishment at the hiss of the Seademon.

The Anglic pointed his arm at the Seademon's ugly, devilish face with the large, staring eye. Its tentacles swept over its head, shining for a moment like a burning crown.

"No," Maeve shouted and brought her helmet down hard on his arm. The gun fired and the water two meters in front of the Seademon spurted up into the air. Maeve was in front of him, clutching with one hand at his gun arm. "No. No."

The Seadragon slid toward them, the water waving away from its powerful chest. There was no time to dodge, only time to throw Maeve to the side as the Seademon reached from the sea. Its long, sinuous tentacles closed about the Anglic's chest and he felt the talons—usually kept in soft pads on the tentacles—sink into his flesh. Then he was flung aside with a twist of its powerful muscles and the hooks raked his body.

Maeve let out a wail like a lost soul. Then she threw herself down beside the Anglic, grunting hysterically. Even now, though, she could not shed tears. Dimly the Anglic could hear shouts from the holding. The large Seademon waved and bobbed in the surf, uncertain what to do about Maeve.

"I'm sorry," the Anglic managed to say. Then the blood bubbled into his lungs and throat. Maeve raised his helmeted head so that he might breathe better. "Go on," he shouted to her. "Go on."

Those were the Anglic's last words. I told the disk to stop when I'd heard our voices, the shouts, the ugly cries of *Witch!* and the sound of the rocks. Slowly I curled my fingers over the disk. "What shall I do with it? Play it for Da?"

"What good would that do?" Caven asked. "Even if he forgave Maeve—which is not likely with your da—the Folk would never have her within the holding again."

"We could play the tape for them too."

"Aye, and they'd call her a demoness and a succubus who misled the Anglic. The Folk will twist any facts to suit their purpose."

120

So we kept the tape, reluctant to destroy the last words of the Anglic. We remained silent during the long eulogy at the Anglic's funeral. There were many who filed past his coffin, respecting the man for what he had been. Even Radog came.

Originally, Da had established the southern edge of the holding as the colony's cemetery; but when the Tearless One was sighted there one night, the Anglic's body was moved to a new set of plots in the hills by his doom. As a precaution, and despite my protests, a stake was driven through the Anglic's heart as well, at the insistence of some of the simpler Folk, lest he become one of the Undead.

And sometimes a lone hunter or fisher would see the Tearless One hunting for his grave along the shore, but she eluded all their darts and fishing spears. Sometimes they would find their nets wrapped around their own boat propellers, and other times their fishing lines would be all tangled. Then they would hear a low, wild laugh. For one moment they would see her astride her one-eyed Seademon, out of the water to her waist, her long hair flowing behind her and the sea spreading out like wings to either side. Then she would be gone.

seven

I

I think of all of us, Athvel took the death of the Anglic the hardest. He thought it was his fault that long ago he had not killed the Tearless One. Besides the Anglic's and Losgann's deaths, he wished the Tearless One dead because, like many of the Folk, he blamed her for the Seademons' new tricks played on the fishers. It had gotten so bad that the fishers refused to put out to sea any more. The Folk regarded such acts as attacks—ignoring the fact, as Phoil ruefully observed, that we were the invaders and the Seademons defending their world in the only way they knew. And Da, of course, took the opportunity to remind Athvel that this was *his* doing, since he was the one who had allowed the Tearless One to come among us. And Folk began recalling Tuathan's words once again, for she seemed to be the fulfillment of the Lady's Curse: more deaths were sure to follow.

I wasn't totally surprised when I saw Athvel stride down the lane to our house wearing leather riding breeches, which were the fashion now. Over his shoulder he had a bundle formed by a rolled-up spacesuit, his crossbow, and a breather pack and helmet.

"I'm off, Ciaran."

"Off to where?" I eased myself down on the bench before our house.

"Da thinks I'm off for a little hunting. But I've a special kind in mind."

"You're after the Tearless One." Caven laid down the needle he had been using to repair a fowling net. "Your da let her stay here. So did we all. It's not your fault about the deaths and the troubles now."

Athvel smiled sardonically. "I'll finish what I started so long ago."

I put my hands to my stomach, feeling the child stirring inside. "I understand the Anglic now. And I understand Losgann. There's something to her that's dark and terrible and yet holds on to the soul. Don't go after her, Athvel."

But Athvel shook his head. "I'll follow her into the very Devil's lair, if I must, to kill the creature."

"And where might that be?"

He laughed lightly. "The Devil's Eyes again. I've a full, scarless cheek that she can have for her canvas."

"Lord, you can't go by yourself," Caven protested. He glanced at me.

"I only came to say goodbye," Athvel insisted. "This task is upon me alone. You're a month from your time, Ciaran. You can't go out into the mountains in the wintertime. And Caven should be here with you."

"Caven'd be of no use when the child's born. He'd just get into the way of the midwives and the rectors."

"The chitters haven't come out yet, Lord. There surely must be one last storm coming. Couldn't you wait, Lord, till the spring?" Caven was torn between his love of Athvel and his love of me. It was a hard thing to love any Devlin.

"And who'll watch his back?" That was a common saying of friendship among the Hounds of Ard-Ri. "You must go with him, Caven."

Caven heaved his shoulders up and down. "If you must go now, I'll go with you, Lord." He went inside the cottage.

Athvel nodded to me. "What will you call the child if it's a boy?"

"Losgann."

"Aye, I thought so." Athvel kissed me lightly and tapped at the corners of my mouth with a finger. "Don't put on such a long face. Even if I don't find Maeve, I'll fetch back some play pretties for the child."

II

It was with a sad heart that I bade goodbye to Ciaran, but there was no gainsaying the Lord's son. In years later they would say the Lord's son knew that his death would soon be upon him; but I, who rode with him, slept beside him, and cooked for him, know otherwise. He was always one with a sad, solemn look.

The fields were bleak and empty yet and the orchard trees were still stripped of any signs of life as we rode out of the holding. And we had ridden no more than a few kilometers when the first heavy flakes began to swirl down.

We took turns at lead after that, for it was wearying work even for stumpies to plow through the deep snowdrifts. Like great, majestic ships of bone and fat and fur, they floundered on, their great breaths rising in huge clouds about their heads.

Spacesuits were ideal outfits to wear in this weather, for they held in the body heat very well—so well that I sweated. We took turns sleeping as well, lashed to our saddles, while the man who stayed awake led the stumpy of the other. When I woke up after one such sleep, I found that the sweat on my stumpy had frozen into ice and there was a small pile of snow. I started to push the snow off and heard a thin, crackling sound. Some snow must have melted on contact with my suit and refrozen into a thin sheet of ice.

All that time the chill mist clung to the black, bare shoulders of the hills so that the dark, frozen fields were lost to view, as if they had never been and only the rocks about us had swum their way out of nothingness, as we edged up the path. Sometimes it seemed like the only solid reality around us was the few meters about each of our stumpies. The great slabs of rock here were stark and terrible and beautiful like the bare bones of this world—as if the mist were like acid stripping away flesh and sinew to purify the soul.

It was already growing dark in the Wailing Mountains, and the sharp-pointed rocks made strange, teeth-like shadows which grew on either side as if jaws were closing about our shadows. There was a strange, lifeless silence here where nothing grew, though sometimes we would hear the high, lonely, keening wind that gave the mountains their name. It was as if we had stumbled over the edge of the world into some strange limbo of the dead, for the Eyes in the wintertime were nothing like in the spring.

After we dismounted, I saw to the hobbling of our stumpies where they would neither be seen nor heard. I left them demolishing a small forest a mile away inland. By the time I made my way back, the Lord had already made camp just below the hill that looked over that one Devil's Eye.

From a sack I took out some of the journeycake and jerky that Ciaran had put in there. I handed a journeycake with a slab of jerky to him.

He sucked absently on a strip of jerky as he gazed at the still, black waters of the Devil's Eye. In the moonlight his scar gleamed like a rune of silver burned into his face—as if the Tearless One had marked the Lord for her own. "Lord, it's in my mind that there are things waking in this Eye, things better left to sleep."

"I've a few surprises for them," he said grimly and unrolled his blanket roll. Within the roll he'd kept a headlamp cannibalized from an abandoned aircar. A hand grip had been welded to the egg-shaped lamp. Wires ran from it to a small power pack which could be attached to his belt.

"Lord, have you ever thought she might have witched you? Have you ever thought she might have drawn you back to here?"

The Lord smiled with a corner of his mouth in his old way. "I thought that by now Ciaran would have knocked all that superstitious nonsense out of you."

"I've little book-learning, if that's what you mean."

The Lord looked at me solemnly. "Brother, there's not another person I'd want by my side in a fight."

"Let it be with the One, then." I watched, puzzled, as he sprayed quick-drying silver reflective paint all over his suit. "Lord, what is that for?"

"You'll see." The Lord set the spray unit down on the rock and held up his suit, inspecting the surface to make sure all the paint had dried. As I started to spray my suit, he climbed into his and fitted his fins over the boots of the suit. "I've kept my eye on you and Ciaran. You've been a good husband to her." He clipped on his weight belt.

"I try to be, Lord," I said.

He was shrugging into his breather pack. "I had no right to take you away from Ciaran at this time." He sat down on the edge of the Eye, dangling his legs in the water. "It was selfish of me."

"You needed me more, Lord." I set the spray unit down and began to slip a leg into my suit.

"You're a brave man, Caven. A good, steady man. I've changed my mind about your coming along. I won't deprive Ciaran and the Folk of a man like you." And saying that, he slipped his helmet over his head, sealing the neck of his suit about the helmet's bottom.

"Lord, what are you—" I tried to stop him, but one leg was in my suit and the other leg out, so I stumbled.

He turned around once again to nod to me and then slid over. I quickly lost sight of his form in the inky black waters, becoming a pale silver blob in only a second which itself vanished the next moment.

126

"Lord, wait for me!" I shouted after him.

Hurriedly I jammed my legs into the suit and reached for my breather pack with one hand even as I reached for my helmet with the other. Out of habit, as Lord Athvel knew I would, I checked the power on the pack and saw the red light that meant the power was all gone. He must have decided several days ago to leave me behind; and secretly, while I was asleep, he must have turned the power pack on, so that it had slowly used up all of its charge. I also found that Lord Athvel had released all the air and the gases—the latter were stored for use at the lower depths. I would have to wait a full day before the sunlight would recharge the pack and pressurize the air, selectively filtering in the necessary gases as well.

As the Lord told me later, he swam down toward the bottom of the Eye slowly, past the skeletal creatures living along its sides, farther than human divers had dared to go before. At the bottom of the pool he found strange, gleaming sticks and rocks of red and blue and orange under his helmet lamp. It was only when he picked them up that he saw they were the skulls and bones of hunters thought lost all these years in the Wailing Mountains. Sea worms and coral growths had covered them. He traveled slowly around the walls at the bottom of the pool, letting his light splash till he found a crack in the wall, shaped curiously like a mouth and with the sides pushed outward like lips as if it were a mouth to the mountains, ready to swallow anyone who dared to enter the pool.

The Lord finished circling the bottom of the pool and found nothing else, so he went back to the crack in the wall. It would be just wide enough for a Seademon to slip through, and so he entered. Immediately it seemed that the passage narrowed so that he could barely squeeze through, his breather pack clonking against the rock wall. He waited for Seademon tentacles to reach out and smash him, but none did. And with slight, careful kicks he gingerly forced his way through. The tunnel twisted and turned, narrowing and then widening over and over so that he felt as if he were in the very belly of the mountains and their intestiny walls were contracting and expanding about him. And perhaps they would contract too much, crushing him.

And though his chronometer counted only an hour or so for the trip, yet it seemed more like an eternity as he probed farther into the passage. Sometimes he would find the cracked shells of crustaceans as if the Seademons often retreated into here and had had some snack during the journey. And once he came across a giant skull—nearly the size of his body—of some lizard-like animal that we did not know. It was turned upside down, and inside the skull were the skeletons of little animals as if the skull were a bowl filled with offerings.

Eventually he came to a fork in the tunnel. In the tunnel to his right lay the remains of a large Seademon, perhaps three meters in length. All that was left now was its skeleton and a harness crudely jeweled with some pearl-like beads. Beside it lay a clumsy club of bone shaped and carved meticulously with running designs. The Lord hesitated, unsure of which tunnel to take, for the one to his right seemed somehow blacker and darker as if it led not out to the sea but outside the universe itself and the large Seademon had been stationed there as some spectral guardian. And yet the Lord felt sure that was the way the Tearless One had gone. Swimming cautiously over the skeleton, the Lord took the passage to his right.

The passage seemed to widen as the Lord swam on. A series of alcoves lined either side. Each alcove held a pile of bones and above each pile was the skull of a Seademon covered with its preserved hide as if it were waiting to be reborn. He rummaged around in the first alcove carefully —the clunking of bones loud in the passage. There seemed to be no bottom to the alcove, as if it were an endless well. After having exposed their dead in the gullies under the sea, the Seademons must have brought their bones here. As the Lord swam by these alcoves, his legs would kick sluggishly as if ghostly tentacles snagged his ankles.

And finally he found himself out on the continental slope, sixteen meters beneath the surface of the sea, which gleamed overhead, silver in the light of the two moons. The surface shifted and twisted under the winds like a sheet of silver being beaten out finer and finer by some smith. The plankton had risen in the sea, so that the black water around him gleamed and sparkled like stars. He chinned the bar that shut off his helmet light and floated there for a time, feeling as if he had drifted away from this world into the starlit sky itself.

And he heard the Tearless One singing, as if from far away, her lost, soulless song that he had heard so long ago. Her voice was unmistakable despite the distortion of sound by the water. With a kick he rose, following the steep-slabbed rock that soared upward to appear as cliffs above the sea. He came to a point where the cliff wall had crumbled into a tumble of rocks and sand that poured itself in a never ending stream down the continental slope toward the sea floor far away.

He took his time moving toward the rocks, trying to watch the wave action, for as the sea entered through the hole in the land's side the water would become flushed for a moment with sparkling plankton stirred up by the wave action, shining and gleaming like some cloud of stars—a cloud that would vanish just as suddenly as it appeared. He counted five quick waves and then a long one. When he thought he had the rhythm of the sea here, he dared to kick in toward the rocks, moving through the sparkling water. Desperately he began to climb upward before a strong wave could rush in, throwing him against the rocks and tearing his suit. When he broke the surface of the sea, he found himself at the mouth of a long, narrow finger of a bay.

It was the neap tide, when the tides were at their lowest. In the regular tides this was a small bay about a half-kilometer across, but now it lay completely exposed. He had to climb three meters up the rocks. Some stream which fed into the bay at high tide ran across the now exposed floor, splashing down the rocks of the slope in a small waterfall. It was easy to find his way in the soft light given off by the coral worms and other animals in the bay above him. The rocks themselves were slippery though, since the trunks and leaves of the blue tri-kelp had collapsed among the lower rocks like kilometers and kilometers of tangled ropes. The barnacles along the cliffs lay exposed, bubbling and frothing and making soft popping noises.

When he reached the floor of the bay, he paused. Before him stood the Devil's moonlit garden. Sponge vases grew, tall and slender. Their flesh within the fine silken webs of glass shone all different colors, gleaming like ghostly pillars. There were giant coral growths like trees twisting in a windstorm. The worms that actually formed the coral trees made soft, slurping sounds as he passed by.

And then he saw the Tearless One, singing to herself as she walked beneath the trees. She was naked; for here, sheltered by the rocks and warmed by the sea, the air was only cool. And the Seademons lay scattered about in the garden, their dark, silent eyes following her as she sang, her voice amplified by the walls of the bay.

Seeing her, the Lord forgot his original intentions. He forgot about the Anglic and about Losgann. He walked forward toward her. She stopped singing. The Seademons turned on their rocks with a sound of wet leather rasping on stone.

With a guttural sound and a clap of her hands, she sent the Seademons slithering across the rocky floor, under the coral trees. Too late, the Lord unclipped the crossbow from where it dangled on his belt. Tentacles coiled about his arms and legs and, struggle as he might, he could not break free. He saw the Tearless One silhouetted against the ghostly garden and then she disappeared over the rocks. In a dark, heaving sea of flesh, the Seademons followed her. Then with a grunt and a rasping breath, the last Seademon let him go. The Lord lifted his crossbow, aiming at the Seademon, which simply turned its back on the Lord contemptuously and slithered back into the sea with a loud splash.

The Lord paused at the edge and thought for a time. Then he walked down the rocks again, entering the bed of tri-kelp. Broad leaves brushed his arms, trying to entangle him, and the trunks undulated and danced like charmed snakes. And then he was free.

For a moment he floated through the eternal darkness, feeling lost. He could not even tell which way was up or down now. Trying to listen, he became aware of his own body—of his breath and his heartbeat. He could smell the sweat of his body within the suit. The entire universe seemed to have vanished, leaving only him.

With his chin he hit the bar that turned on the infrared scanner in his helmet. The outer face of the helmet's visor acted like a lens, feeding information through a scanner that then flashed the images onto the rear of the visor, which served as a screen. The layers of crystals between the front and rear sides of the helmet visor would grow opaque and even black in the meantime.

The undersea world suddenly burned in ghostly outline before his eyes. He found he had gotten himself turned upside down, so that the continental slope seemed to be above his head as if it were some muddy roof trying to trap him. He straightened himself so that the surface of the sea was overhead as it should be. Then he moved down the slope, entering the world of dreams, the land of night-

131

mares. It was almost as if he were not moving, but standing still while the world changed about him. And then the Seademons, their bodies flaming with heat like torches, drifted toward him.

He clipped his crossbow back onto his belt and slipped the high-power headlight off of it. Then he chinned off the infrared scanner, putting himself back into that almost total darkness, before he snapped on the headlight. In the blackness the beam of light seemed almost tangible, as if it were a lance. He caught a Seademon floating with eyes unlidded; and he shone the point of the light beam full on its eyes. The eyes shone bright with the unnatural light for a moment and then it shot away in terror and in pain. He caught three other Seademons, blinding them with the intense light so that they swam about in panic, blundering into each other; and the rocks of the slope echoed their shrill whistles.

With a kick, the Lord swam as fast as he could down the slope. One moment it seemed that his light caught a giant scarlet circle. It seemed almost solid; but as he swam closer, the circle dissolved into thousands of red bodies of Seademons darting about in confusion.

Bright as the sun seemed the headlight—or a star, fallen into the sea. To the Seademons it must have seemed like the end of the world. He set the lamp even higher, risking using up the lamp filaments or battery. With satisfaction, he noticed that the light shone from his specially painted suit as if the suit were a mirror. Even to his own vision, he seemed to have changed into a ball of fire.

He swam to where they seemed the densest. Bodies slammed into him accidentally, and he found it hard to swim in their current. Then the pack of darting, panicked bodies disappeared, leaving only the large, venerable, one-eyed Seademon. And with her legs wrapped around its back, the slim, suited figure of the Tearless One.

He polarized his visor and released the little bombs that

132

were clipped to the back of his belt. They exploded, releasing clouds of fine metal foil into the water. Once used to confuse enemy detection devices during a jump, they burned in the light of the lamp like thousands of stars which he saw only dimly through his polarized visor.

The giant Seademon lay stunned, twisting its body this way and that, as if it could shake off its blindness, and the Tearless One clung desperately to its back, her arms wrapped around its neck, her legs now flailing in the water. He threw the net bombs—spheres which shot out small jets that trailed nets behind them, the last in our arsenal. They were meant for other uses than capturing the Tearless One.

The Seademon and the Tearless One writhed in the tight elastic mesh. The white plastic flashed as if they were caught in nets of fire. The Lord held her through the mesh and she kicked and wriggled as best she could. He sprayed the harmless agent onto certain strands of the net so that they dissolved, leaving the Tearless One still partly bound. Drawing her after him, he swam away from the Seademon which began to burble in an alarmed way. Already the powerful tentacles of the Seademon had forced their way through holes of the mesh tearing or stretching many of the strands. The Lord turned the headlight as bright as he dared, the water hissing and steaming before the lens.

They were near the surface when the light failed. He threw the now useless headlamp and power pack away. The Tearless One pulled free at that moment and, to the Lord's surprise, swam beside him up the slope, the frantic gurgling of the Seademons already growing louder. They splashed out of the water among the rocks, decompressing inside their suits, moving stiffly like bloated rubber dolls.

Over his suit radio the Lord spoke to her: "I came to kill you." He sprayed the net with the solvent, and the remaining strands rotted and fell away into harmless organic foam that slid down her suit to the ground. The Lord slipped his fins off his lightweight boots. "Now we're going to climb."

But the Tearless One stayed where she was, wiping at the foam on her suit. "If the Lord wishes to kill Maeve, let him do it now."

"Are you afraid of me?"

"Yes. Is the Lord afraid of Maeve?"

"Yes. Now climb."

They climbed up the rocks. The sea had risen slightly, covering the floor of the bay now; but up above the cliffs they were reasonably safe. Once there, he radioed to me to meet him. Then the Lord waited, saying nothing until it was time to take off his helmet. He signed for her to do the same.

She unsealed the collar and slipped off her helmet, shaking her hair free. It was long and black and the tangled curls clung to the wet shoulders of her suit. As she had grown older, her cheekbones had become harder and more prominent. She looked even more like some creature of the wild.

"Why doesn't the Lord kill Maeve?"

Lord Athvel sat back and laughed. "I don't know, really. Except that I thought no harm should come to such a lovely creature as you."

The Tearless One ran her fingers lightly across the visor of her helmet. "Don't make funny sounds."

"I don't risk the Seademons to make a joke." Lord Athvel rubbed his chin. "But why did you come with me when you'd pulled free?"

"Maeve does not know." The Tearless One looked at him with an odd, unreadable expression. "The Lord is either a very brave man or a fool."

"I'm told I'm a little of both."

"And pretty too."

She ran a finger down the front of her suit, unsealing it. She shrugged first one arm and the other out of the sleeves. Her breasts were small and round and her waist was long and slender, flaring out to wide hips. She stood up and pulled off her suit. Then she knelt before

134

him and unsealed his suit. The Lord let himself be led through the rocks into a cave in the mountains behind them. Like a fox or marten, she seemed to see with night eyes, walking without stumbling or hesitating. Then she stopped where she had made a bed of aromatic moss—as if she used this cave for sleeping sometimes. With a smile, she made him sit down on the moss. Her touch was child-like and yet hurried.

It was I who woke them the next day as I climbed along the clifftops, calling to the Lord. He came out, holding her hand.

The Lord took the string of cringies from my hand. "Good man. We're famished."

"Hello, Caven Wilderman," the Tearless One called out gaily.

I nodded cautiously. "Good day to you." I skinned the cringies and roasted them; for the Lord and the Tearless One were too much caught up in one another. It seemed almost as if she had bewitched him, but the Lord must ever be after something new, and that was what led to his downfall, truly. We waited nearly a week with me camping outside the cave. Beneath the cliff we could hear the Seademons snuffling and howling mournfully. The Tearless One only smiled as if she were amused.

"What are they saying?" the Lord asked.

"They think Athvel is the Sun Demon," she laughed. "They think Athvel is the one who hurts their eyes so much in the daytime. They think the Sun Demon has stolen Maeve."

Finally, at the end of the eighth day, the Lord came out alone from the cave mouth. The Tearless One was still asleep. "What are you going to do with the Tearless One?" I asked.

"Why, take my lovely lady home, of course."

"She'll be burned at the stake," I said.

"The Folk wouldn't dare."

"Only if your da forbade it. And he won't."

"*I'd* forbid it, then. The Folk would listen to me."

"Lord, you're thinking with your heart and not your head."

"She's as human as you or I. Maybe even more so."

"Be that as it may, she wouldn't last out the night if you were to take her back to the holding now."

After a moment the Lord shrugged. "Then I won't take her back."

"What will you do?"

"We'll start our own holding here."

"Turn your back on the Folk?"

"Aye, and be happy about it." The Lord smiled in a free and easy way I'd never seen before. "For once I can be myself and not the Lord's Sorrow."

"But you're our future Lord," I protested.

"If they won't have my lady, I won't have *them.*" He spoke with a suddenly boyish breeziness.

"Lord," I said earnestly, "think about what you are saying. For the good of your soul, remember what happened to those others who fell in love with her."

The Lord pulled at the rayed circle that hung about his neck. Its leather thong broke with a snap and he pitched the medallion over the cliff. "It was only through their own stupidity that they came to harm. I won't."

It hurt me to say what I had to next. "Then let me go home, Lord. It will be spring soon. Let me go back to your sister and her child if they live."

Lord Athvel cocked his head. The chitters were still making the high, scratching sounds that were their mating calls. A few of them had strayed into the few plants that grew hereabouts. "How long have the chitters been here?"

"The last few nights."

"I lost track of time. Of course you can go." He held my

136

shoulder and gave me a shake. "And don't worry about me, Caven. I'm happy. For the first time in my life, I'm truly happy."

And at the time he seemed so.

eight

I

A true year passed and it was April again, but now our world was deep in winter. The snow lay in heavy drifts along the passes and all the Folk had bundled themselves away into their homes. But in the middle of the night we heard a pounding at the door. I took my crossbow from its peg on the wall and covered Caven while he tilted back the bar and swung the door in.

A lone figure, covered with snow, stood in the doorway. Behind him, a dim blur in the falling snow, we could see the silhouette of a shivering stumpy. He stepped inside, twisting his helmet off from the neck of his suit.

"Athvel!" I said in surprise.

"Aye." He grinned. He was tall and gaunt and there was a haunted look to him. "The prodigal returneth. Won't someone kill the fatted calf?"

I ran to him then and hugged him. Even through his bulky suit I could feel how thin he was. At the same time Caven began to pound him on the back.

"Easy, easy," Athvel gasped. "I've not come all this way to be beaten to death."

While Caven and Athvel put his stumpy in the pen, I added fuel to the fire so that it was roaring by the time they returned.

I handed Athvel a cup of brandy, but he did not drink it,

preferring to walk over to little Losgann's cradle.

"He looks just like Losgann when he was that age," Athvel said.

"Does he? I wasn't sure."

Athvel downed his brandy in one gulp. "By the One, that's good. You don't know how good something is until you can't have any."

I took the cup from his hand and refilled it from the jar. "Just don't try to make up for all those dry months in a few wet minutes."

"Oh, I'd almost forgotten." Athvel unsealed the front of his suit and took out a small rattle made from a crawler shell, but it was a species that I'd never seen, the shell being a bright red instead of the familiar blue of the crawlers hereabouts. The six leg holes had been filled in and some pebbles rattled inside. A stick, thrust into one of the neck holes, would let the baby shake it. "A play-pretty," Athvel said. "Maeve made it."

I took it. "It was very thoughtful of her."

But Athvel saw Caven's scowl. "You can have the rectors de-witch it for you." He strode over to the fireplace and spread his legs. The steam began to rise from his suit and boots. He finished his second cup before he spoke again, keeping his eyes on the flames all the while. "There's no use mincing words with you. I came to ask your help, Ciaran."

"What kind of help? We've plenty of food—"

"Not that kind. Maeve is pregnant."

"How wonderful," I said unenthusiastically.

"I want our child born in the holding. The rectors and midwives can do so much more for Maeve than I could. She's such a small thing, after all." Athvel took the jar from me and poured himself a third cup. "Will you help me, Ciaran?"

"How many months is the Te— I mean, Maeve?"

"Five months."

"And you came through a snowstorm to tell us? It could have waited."

"You're right. I've not told you all." Athvel hid his face behind his brandy cup for a moment. "She's been talking to the Seademons again. They're terribly angry because she left them for me—they know I'm no Sun Demon now. She's had to strike some kind of bargain with them that she won't tell me about, but she mopes around all day." Athvel looked at me suddenly. His eyes seemed as sad and wise as Da's now. "I'm afraid for her, Ciaran. She may go wild again."

I had understood Athvel and forgiven him; and Mihangel and Cularen had forgiven him, though they did not understand. There was only Da to deal with. If we could win Da to our side, the Folk would probably leave her alone. I sighed. "Well, I want Losgann in Da's arms before I begin talking. Grandparents get greedy that way, you know."

"I knew I could count on you, little sister." Athvel set his cup down on the mantel. "And now tell me all the news and gossip I've missed. . . ."

The next evening I had Da over to our house for dinner. He sat in a chair before the fireplace, listening to the winds howl outside. Caven lounged on the floor before the fire, warming the brandy in his stomach.

"Do you know," I said, "the snow must be four feet deep outside."

Da only grunted, cradling Losgann while I began to read to him, the pages flashing slowly over the surface of the reader's cube. Suddenly Da interrupted me in mid-sentence. "Do you think it's snowing heavily in the mountains by the sea?" He'd been fretting like this all the time Athvel had been gone.

"I suppose," I said. "Especially if you're on the landward side of the mountains without a great big ocean to warm you." I went back to reading, but a minute later Da interrupted again.

"I suppose that fool had enough sense to stock fuel in his cave."

"Athvel's capable, Da," I said, "even if you'd never admit it."

Da slouched back in his chair. Two minutes later he swung one leg up, crossing it over the other. "Do you think he has much food?"

"He has the whole sea," I said.

"And Seademons to bedevil him all the time."

I snapped off the cube. "Then fetch him back in chains, but don't sit about wondering all the time."

"No." Da crossed his arms firmly. "He brought this all upon himself."

"Da, are you punishing Athvel or yourself? All this time I thought you were trying to hurt Athvel, but you've really been trying to punish yourself by bullying the one living person you love the most."

"What kind of talk is that?" Da grumbled. "I've whipped people who have said less than that to me."

"Well, go on," I said. I took Losgann from Da and put him in Caven's arms. "I'm a true Hound of Ard-Ri now."

Da shook his head. "Be off with you. I've nearly fifty kilos on you and I'm at least a head taller."

"And I'm younger and faster and scrappier. Or are you scared, Da?"

"I'm going to spank some sense into you as I should have before." Da rose, tipping over his chair. He rolled back his sleeves ominously.

I had started to drape my shawl over the back of my chair when Da rushed me, arms outstretched, meaning to catch me by surprise and end the fight with one of his big bear hugs. But I'd been expecting him to cheat. I sidestepped, blocked his right arm as he swung it in to grab me, and then

I kicked his legs just behind the knees. His great legs buckled underneath him. I held on to his right arm as he went down and twisted it around behind him. He fell heavily on his knees. I kicked him in his back and he crashed forward on his face. I clambered onto his back, holding his right arm behind him. He tried to push himself from the ground, the sinews standing out on his neck and arms like cords. His face contorted in pain as he tried to rise. I tell you, it was a little like trying to ride the sea.

"Is this what you're really afraid of?" I asked. "Are you afraid Athvel will take everything from you? Is that why you've hounded him so?"

Da stopped at that and lay panting on the floor. "Ciaran, you get to be more and more like your mother every day. She was a good woman, but a scold."

"Someone has to watch you, Da." I got up.

He rose slowly, rubbing his arm admiringly. "At least there's one fighter in the family."

"Da, you're starting it again."

He grinned sheepishly. "So I am. Well, come the thaw, we'll go looking for our stray lamb."

"You don't really need to, Da," I said. "Athvel, come in now."

Athvel came in from the side room we used for storage. "Good evening, sir."

Da turned several shades of red, working into deeper hues of purple. He glared first at Athvel and then at me. "Betrayed," he bellowed.

"Be quiet," I snapped, "and sit down."

Da wagged his finger at me. "You have more respect for me."

"I will when you start showing some sense."

"How dare you—"

"Sit down," I outshouted him. "Or Caven and I will pack up Losgann and leave the holding too." Da shut his mouth more from astonishment than from anything else. It was my turn to wag my finger at him. "Now, all of us have put up with your shouting and your tantrums about as much as we can. It's time for you to start acting like a grown man again."

Da shifted his feet uncomfortably, staring down at the floor. "Well—" he cleared his throat—"do you want to come back, Athvel?"

"Aye."

"And the Tearless One?"

"I'll bring her back with me. She's with child."

Da looked up, startled. "Are you crazy, man? You can't bring her among the Folk pregnant. They'll be even more likely to burn her."

"Sir, she's such a small thing. I'm afraid to let her have her child out in the wilderness. I'm sure there's going to be trouble."

Da pursed his lips and clapped his hands together softly while he thought. "Birthing's none too easy," he agreed, perhaps remembering Athvel's mother. "Would she agree to go through any ceremonies that Phoil might hold to purify her?"

"She'll agree, Da."

"Then if I speak to a few people, I think we can save her from the stake." Da got up suddenly and, with more warmth than he had ever shown to Athvel before, he gave Athvel a quick, clumsy hug. "Welcome home, then."

II

The Folk were none too easy in their minds about having the Tearless One back, even though Prime Rector Phoil held a week of ceremonies to cleanse her. The Tearless One bore all this with much more patience and good humor than I expected; but then Athvel stayed by her side all the while, insisting that he go through the same purification rites as she did. And it was obvious to anyone with eyes

143

that they were very much in love with one another.

At first things went well. Athvel and the Tearless One stayed within one of the many rooms in Doom Devlin so that the Tearless One had little contact with the Folk. But then, when it was eight months into the Tearless One's term, the first Seademon appeared on the beach. It did not attack the watch, but merely stared at them accusingly until they shot it. The next night a second Seademon appeared. It was killed. The third night another Seademon came and the watch no longer bothered to drag the body away but dug a hole in the sand, covering it with a layer of lye followed by a layer of sand. It was as if the Seademons wished to show their contempt—a contempt for death rather than for us since we seemed beneath even their contempt. When ten Seademons had died, they stopped coming.

Although the Tearless One had been happy enough before this, she became quiet and withdrawn when she heard about the Seademons. Athvel and I began to take turns with her, never leaving her alone for a moment; for she began to speak strangely, as if the child she carried were sired not by Athvel but by the sea. It was the sea's child, she would say, and due the sea. And when asked what she meant, she would only shake her head desperately and claim that she had promised never to tell.

It was a difficult childbirth. The Tearless One slipped from the Folk's tongue back into Lugashkemi, so that the midwives were constantly touching Earthstuff and moving it in Sane Collen's sign for protection. And the Tearless One went beyond even that into the language of her earliest childhood, a strange tongue that Phoil said was one of the tongues of old Tara, the language of Hy Brasil. At that point the midwives—as much as they respected the Prime Rector—would not come back to the bed to help the Tearless One until Phoil threatened them with Alienation from the Folk.

Still, it was well for the Tearless One that the child

144

looked like Athvel and was not some horned monster or both she and her baby would have been destroyed.

I washed him with my own hands—only Phoil and I would touch him—and wrapped him in a blanket I had woven myself. "He's a fine boy, Maeve." I held him up for her to see. "What will you call him?"

The Tearless One blinked at me and her eyes seemed to focus only gradually as if she were only just now becoming aware of me.

"Maeve, you have a boy. What will you name him?"

"The sea will name him." The Tearless One rolled her head around on the pillow to look away from him. She sounded tired not just in body but to the very core of her soul.

We were all a bit puzzled by the Tearless One's attitude toward the child; but when she refused to name him—though it was her prerogative—Athvel did, calling the boy Iriel after one of the early Devlins. And for an entire true year after that the Tearless One fed Iriel as if it were some embarrassing task she had to perform, putting the child to her breasts mechanically and without caring. But to Athvel she remained as loving—if a bit guarded now—as ever.

We were surprised, then, when we found her down by the beach. Both members of the watch had been knocked out by the old stunner that lay by her knee in the sand, and the beach all about the Tearless One was covered with the tracks of Seademons.

"Where's Iriel?" I asked her.

The Tearless One began to rock back and forth on the sand. She pulled her shawl tighter about her shoulders to hide her swollen breasts. The milk began staining the wool. "He's the sea's child now."

I could only stare at her in horror. "What do you mean?"

"The Bearer must have her due."

"The Bearer?"

The Tearless One struggled for the proper words in our

language. "The Great One. The Old One. The Source." She glanced nervously up at us and then back to the sea. "They told Maeve all this before Athvel brought her here. But Maeve can say no more. She promised she would not even say this much."

I knelt beside the Tearless One, trying to put my arms around her; but she shrank away from my touch. I dropped my hands uselessly into my lap. "You mean you gave your child to the Seademons?"

"They will feed him on the milk of Tritons. Maeve has drunk it. It is very rich. He will grow strong in the sea."

"But he'll drown."

"Maeve has thought it all out. She has stolen all kinds of diving skins and other things. Maeve's friends will know what to do." Her last sentence sounded so final.

"How could you give up your own child to them?" I demanded.

The Tearless One turned then to look at me and Athvel and the others. Her eyes had a strange, faraway look, and I shivered and had to hold myself. I saw that if she were human, it was not as we understood the word.

"Ciaran's folk do not know what powers and forces lie beneath the waves. It was to keep them from becoming angry that Maeve gave them the child. He was payment for the lives of Ciaran and Athvel's Folk . . . for taking Maeve from the sea. From them." Her eyes appealed silently to Athvel. "It was something Maeve had to do to be free. Now all her other children will belong to the land."

Athvel's hands clenched and unclenched. "And what will you do with them? Bury them alive in sand or throw them on the rocks?"

The Tearless One turned awkwardly on her knees. "Maeve will love them, of course, and raise them and cherish them, because they will belong to Maeve and to Athvel and not to the sea." She reached her hand out toward Athvel.

Athvel stared down at her hand as if it were leprous. "Monster they called you and monster you are. We shall never touch again." And he spun about on his heel and stalked up the beach, and the others left one by one until the Tearless One and I were sitting alone on the sands.

III

We tried to summon the Seademons to parley, but it was as if they had vanished. Athvel took it badly, sitting and brooding all the time, speaking only when he wanted more whiskey. He had angrily rebuffed the Tearless One's few pitiful attempts to talk to him, and then it was her turn to become angry and silent.

And then on one November night—hot and muggy with this world's summer—Mihangel pounded desperately on our door. I sat up sleepily, drawing the fur blanket about me while Caven drew back the door, knife in one hand. Mihangel stood gasping and leaning against the doorway.

"Ciaran," he called to me, "you've always had a way with him. See if you can't talk some sense into him now."

"Sense into who?" I reached my hand out and found my shift.

"Athvel. He's for going off to the Seademons' lairs and winning back his son, though how he's to talk to them is beyond even him."

"The grief has driven him mad," Caven said.

"More like that witch." Mihangel spat into the fireplace. "Curse the day we ever set eyes upon her." He went outside while I dressed. Caven sat by the cradle, silently watching me. Since the theft of Iriel, no parents left their children unguarded. It was a mindless, unreasoning fear, and yet one that no one laughed at or dared defy.

"He's right, you know. One of us should have stuck a knife into her a long time ago. Not that she's a witch, but she's as bad as one for what she's done to us."

"As for that, the fault's more in our minds than in her doings," I threw back. I laced on my sandals. Caven held out my cloak and slipped it over my shoulders.

Mihangel and I set off for the doom at a steady jog.

"Has Athvel spoken to the Tearless One?"

"Aye, that's the trouble." Mihangel was already puffing heavily. His wife, an ample woman herself, inclined to overfeed him. "He threw down his cup tonight and stormed into her room. They shouted at each other for a bit, and when he came out, his face was all pale and his mouth shut tight and his eyes wild."

"What could she possibly have said to him?"

"She must be a witch," Mihangel said with firm conviction.

I went to the Tearless One's bedroom as soon as I got to Doom Devlin—since that terrible night when we lost Iriel, she and Athvel had not slept in the same room. I squatted down in the tunnel and knocked. The Tearless One jerked open the door in the metal frame. She stared at me with a mixture of surprise and hostility.

"What does Ciaran want?"

"What did you say to Athvel that's driven him nearly as mad as Losgann?"

"He does not understand. None of Ciaran's folk have understood."

"Understood what?" I demanded.

The Tearless One hesitated and then shook her head. "Maeve will never tell. Never again."

"Maeve, Athvel says he's going to fetch back Iriel."

"He is?" The Tearless One thought for a moment, looking as if she wanted to go out; but then perhaps she remembered something particularly harsh that Athvel had said to her. Her mouth pressed itself into a firm, bloodless line. "He is a fool."

"Maeve, won't you come with me? Won't you help me talk him out of this madness?"

"He said he would kill Maeve if he ever saw her again."
And regretfully but resolutely, the Tearless One closed her
door.

I heard a yell and a crash as I re-entered the great hall.
I pushed my way through the mob before the tunnel leading into Athvel's room. I found him standing in the middle
of the room, a chair leg in either hand and the rest of the
chair broken over Da's back and head. I dropped to my
knees beside Da and brushed some of the stuff away, feeling his neck. "There's a strong pulse still."

"Thank the One," Athvel said. He threw the chair legs
away. I went to his bed and picked up the diving suit. It had
been coated with silver paint again. And by it were another
headlight and power pack.

"You'll not fool the Seademons twice with the same
trick," I warned.

"I'll just go among them and make signs. I've watched
Maeve."

"We won't let you go, Athvel," I said.

Athvel proceeded to roll his things into a bundle. "I'd
like to see the man or woman who could stop me."

I placed myself between Athvel and the door. "Help
me," I appealed to Mihangel and Cularen. They joined me,
pressing against me on either side as if we were a human
wall.

Athvel tied the straps around his bundle. Without raising
his head, he said, "In the event that Da is incapacitated, I
rule in his stead."

"That's in case of illness, not for when you hit him over
the head." I glanced at Mihangel and Cularen, both of
whom grunted their support.

"He had an accident." Athvel added the bundle to the
rest of his diving gear and shouldered it all. "He ran into
the chair in my hands." He eyed the three of us and started
forward, but we would not budge. Athvel looked at us
earnestly, each in turn. "I think I understand why the

Seademons claimed Iriel. If I can communicate with them, I might be able to explain that they're wrong and fetch him back. But you must take my word for it when I tell you it's not something to be spoken of."

"What possible reason could you have?" I asked. "Do you think we'll let you go to your death—yes, it's your death, Athvel, and don't deny it—do you think we'll let you do that without knowing the reason why?"

"If you love me, sister, don't make me tell."

"You won't tell me because there is no such reason." I folded my arms across my stomach.

Athvel stepped back, refusing to look at any of us. He tried to sound off-hand and casual, but there was a brittle edge to his voice. "Maeve'd stick most anything inside herself, you know." He pretended to ignore our shocked faces and gasps of disbelief. Instead he gave a little laugh. "They probably think the lad is theirs."

Mihangel and Cularen stood for a moment in an agony of indecision. Cularen was the first to break. "Cularen!" I said in alarm. I clutched at his sleeve.

"A person must do what he or she must," Cularen said with pig-headed stubbornness. And he pulled his arm away. If I had held on to his sleeve, he would have dragged me along with him to the side, so I had to let go.

"Aye, Athvel must do what he can," Mihangel said. I turned around to see him moving to the other side. I reached for him too late. My hand grasped at the empty air. Only I remained in Athvel's way.

"You can't judge her conduct by our standards," I tried to argue. "She was raised differently than we were, so what are our sexual rules to her? She thinks of humanity more broadly than we do."

"And what of my son, your nephew? Would you have him raised by those monsters? Perform whatever abominable acts they perform in the darkness?" Despite all of his learning and cynicism and Da's training—perhaps even because of it—Athvel preferred thinking with his heart and not his head when it came to the most important things.

"We don't even know if he's still alive." I finally spoke aloud the thought that everyone had been afraid to say before this.

Hurt and angry, Athvel looked at me. "I must know, Ciaran, if he's dead or alive."

"Athvel, think of the Folk if you won't think of us, your family."

He gave my shoulders a squeeze. And I saw his death in his eyes, for he had loved a Maeve that had never existed and he had just discovered this night how wrong he had been. "I must live out my mother's curse."

"Wait a moment and we'll go with you," Mihangel said.

Athvel half turned. "No, this journey is laid only upon me. I will kill whatever person tries to follow me."

"Even me?" I asked.

"Even you, little sister," he said and gave me one of his sardonic smiles. And the Folk would say later that his light-ness came from being enchanted by the Sea Witch, but I say it was because he simply wanted to die. He crawled through the doorway and the tunnel. The crowd of guards and servants on the other side parted for him. No one tried to stop him, for there was a terrible splendor to him as he walked away to fulfill the destiny his mother had pro-nounced for him.

It was the last we saw of Athvel.

IV

When Athvel was alive, Da had been inclined to bully and abuse him the way you misuse something you are afraid you may love too much—love so much that you never want it to grow closer to you for fear of the love becoming over-whelming, or because you may lose it. Da did not realize this until Athvel was gone, and then it was too late. And in his madness and grief Da let loose the Hounds of Ard-Ri to harry the Seademons in their very lairs; for either Iriel would be given back to us or he would be killed by the Seademons—which we thought a better fate than to be raised by such creatures.

The sound of the pipes and drums was like the strongest whiskey to the Folk. The veterans were recapturing their youth; the young Folk wanted to match their parents' deeds. Robots were re-programed for war by the rectors and Mihangel. Ammunition was broken out of storage and given away freely while weapons were stripped, cleaned, and oiled. All day long I and the other commanders trained alongside our companies.

The entire colony literally hummed day and night as we worked to prepare jerky and journeycakes. All the spare metal was melted down to make sword blades, spear points, halberd and ax heads. The younger Hounds had to serve as crossbowmen since the old rapid-fire weapons that would work underwater had been given to the trusted veterans who knew how to use them. Clothes and boots were patched and repaired. Even the children were kept busy.

I was making up a little kit of Losgann's things, for Da had ordered me to command the garrison troops at home since I was now his heir; but I was damned if I was going to be left behind. I intended to stand with the rest of the garrison troops and wave goodbye to Da—and, as soon as Da was out of sight, leave Losgann with Cularen's wife and join my company on the march. After all, I had been trained to lead my company. Caven would be by my side as well. On the day of our marriage he had transferred to my company from the company Athvel had commanded.

I had grown used to the war sounds—boots tramping up and down the lane and equipment belts jingling at all hours of the day and night; the running, the shouting, and always the edge of eagerness to the voices like the edge I always imagined would be there in the voices of hunting dogs when they'd caught the scent of their quarry and begun to bay. It might have been a little quieter if I had moved into Doom Devlin again as Da wanted, but I'd grown used to the privacy of our own cottage, so I had refused to move.

And then suddenly the noise came to a stop outside. My one concession to my new status had been to take Eriu, now a boot, as my maid. She left Losgann tottering about to go to the door. I joined her there. The men and women in the lane had frozen still; and moving among them as if they were not there at all was the Tearless One, dressed in a long skirt whose hem was now dusty.

She had really risked her life when she left the protection of her room. More than one hand touched the hilt of a knife. The Tearless One had a guard of two Hounds, but they were to prevent her from escaping, not to protect her. Her death would have relieved them of a very unpopular duty.

I opened the gate and motioned her inside the house. "Watch the outside," I told Eriu. With an uncertain glance at the Tearless One, Eriu placed herself in front of the door as I shut it. The Tearless One looked at the traveling packs being made ready and the slabs of smoked meat hanging from the ceiling.

"Ciaran must stop them," the Tearless One said. "Ciaran's Folk do not know the powers of this world."

"What powers, Maeve?"

The Tearless One pushed at a slab of jerky, watching it spin slowly around on its string. "Maeve . . . Maeve mustn't say. Maeve promised long ago never to tell. But there are forces, great forces that have little to do with the ways of Ciaran's Folk but are quick to anger when disturbed. And not all the guns and rockets of the Folk can stop them."

I suddenly became aware again of how small the Tearless One was, for the jerky hung just about at the level of my mouth and the Tearless One had to look up to it. "Poor Maeve, you never really understood us, did you? You never realized what we can and will do when we are angry."

And it was as if something within the Tearless One that had been bending, bending inside like a reed, had now snapped. "It's Ciaran's Folk who do not understand. If something or someone does not do what the Folk want, the Folk kill it. The Folk think they must conquer this world or be conquered. They think it weakness to make any changes to live with this world."

"What changes have the Seademons made? They've been stubborn—"

"They let Maeve come back. It is unknown among them for females, the Bearers, to live side by side with the Bringers, the males. If Maeve had had a daughter, she might have been able to stay with Maeve."

"You said the Bearer must have her due."

"Athvel took Maeve from the sea. She had to be replaced."

"So even if it had been a girl child, you might not have been allowed to keep her."

"No," the Tearless One said reluctantly, "Maeve might not have been allowed."

"Do the Seademons think the child is theirs?"

"Maeve tried to tell Athvel why the child belonged to the sea. And she told him more things than he could accept; for, like all of his Folk, he was small-minded."

"If you think I'll let some beastly alien take hold of me, you're mistaken."

The Tearless One smiled strangely. "That is funny. That is what many of Maeve's friends say about Ciaran's folk." She looked up at me then with an unshakable certainty. "Maeve belongs to this world in ways that Ciaran will never know."

"You are a witch," I said. "Truly a witch, to give yourself in such a worldly way."

"The things of this world are natural. Which one is unnatural—Ciaran or Maeve?" She turned without another word and started out the door, moving without hesitation past Eriu toward the sullen crowd gathered in the lane. Her guard had disappeared, leaving her to her fate. I hesitated for a moment, so I had to hurry in order to join her. Eriu tried to stop me, but I pushed her away. If I had not been by the side of the Tearless One, she would not have lived beyond the gate. As it was, we walked side by side without a word; and I left her side only when we reached the doom. I watched her enter the softly glowing interior. Her guard, frowning at finding her still alive, flanked her on either side.

V

It was a rousing sight to see the Folk marching to war. The old, grizzled veterans, their faces tanned by a hundred suns and scarred by as many alien weapons, rode in the stumpy carts. Beside them, marching in their slow, steady, ground-eating pace, were the Shippies and Worldlies.

And slung over their shoulders and dearer to them than life itself were their weapons—a quartermaster's nightmare: crossbows, darters, and even crude rifles that fired bullets from a chemical explosion. Their stocks and triggers were not originally designed for human hands, since they were part of our loot from the Long Flight. They would be used by those who remained ashore. The older Hounds might have some of our precious power rifles that would work underwater.

Canteens clinked and helmets slung behind on backs bobbed up and down, rattling against the metal parts of travel packs. And there would be the low, mournful bellowing of supply stumpies goaded along by their drivers. And the regimental pipers managed to find the breath to skirl the tunes of "Garry Owen" and "Lie Down, Tarans, Lie Down," "The Clan Keogh," and even "Men of Harlech"—

the last the only thing that drew a smile from Caven.

And it seemed at that moment that no one could stop the Hounds of Ard-Ri.

They did not come the first day when we took one stone away from their temple, so the next day we took two, lifting them from the sea by cables hooked to a flotilla of straining aircars and dropped them unceremoniously on a plateau where they were to be kept for ransom. Though, during the nighttime, some of the Folk had carved insulting, obscene pictures into the stone surfaces or simply urinated on them; for a sullen anger was growing among the Folk. When the scouts had entered the temple, they had found human skulls set into newly carved niches in the upright stones— none of them was Athvel's, for the rectors knew his teeth. And the skins of the humans had been taken off their bodies and carefully preserved and the flesh of the head had been pulled back over the skull, leaving the rest of the hide to dangle down like the cloak from a hood. Phoil suspected they had been placed there as some kind of guardian. More and more, though, I heard rumors among the Hounds that the men and women had been skinned alive—even though no one knew for sure. But there were neat little holes driven into the skulls as if someone had wanted to eat the brains first. It did not leave the Hounds in a pleasant mood after they had seen their dead treated that way.

Today we would take three stones.

The sea was a reddish brown, the color of drying blood, but here and there the plankton gathered in patches, staining the surface with circles of iridescent red and purple— as if they were the eyes of a peacock's tail and the whole of the heaving sea were a fan waving the harsh, sunlit dreams away from the land. But beneath the peacock's tail the real face of our world, smiling darkly as a houri, hid herself with the coming of light.

A flare went off, burning bright as a red star in the air for a moment as it whirled about slowly, suspended from a small anti-gravity disk. Around us, the men and women of my company stirred, looking to their weapons.

"If they wait much longer, they'll have no temple left," Caven said to me.

Ferdie Manamar, uncle to Eriu, sat next to Caven. "They might come, but not too far." Ferdie checked over the power pack that charged his rifle. "They'll be wanting us to meet them—like the Xh'lch at Osanla."

Eriu turned around so suddenly that the long braid of her scalp lock thumped softly against her breather pack— she still had not grown used to having such long hair. "I thought they were on a mountaintop there. And we had enough aircars to land on top and drive them down. What are we going to do here?"

"You just think in reverse, d'you see?" And the two fell into a lengthy discussion of tactics, fighting and refighting battles which had happened even before the old Hound had been born; for the battles of the Ninth were stories that one grew up with, so that a child could sometimes recite the order of the units in some famous battle before the child could tell you the entire alphabet.

I wished I could get absorbed in such a conversation. It might distract me from the heat inside the spacesuit. The cooling system in the suit wasn't geared to keeping you comfortable, only alive. Even taking your helmet off only gave some relief; but I had kept my helmet on to monitor commands. Caven cupped his hand over his mouth, leaned forward until his hand touched my helmet, and shouted— though his voice only came thin and hollow through the helmet wall: "I still say you ought to tell your da that you're here!"

"This is my company! What were all those years of training for?" I shouted back. "Captain Ian can tell Da the truth after the fight: that I threatened the poor captain with all types of punishments if he informed on me."

Caven made a sharp, impatient, clicking sound with his tongue.

Beside us sat the faithful Ardui, who by some conspiracy had been detached from his own squad in the company and attached to me as my bodyguard. "I'll stay with the Lady Ciaran no matter what, Caven," he said matter-of-factly.

"And I," said Eriu.

"See that you do," Caven warned the both of them.

I was about to tell them that I was quite capable of looking after myself when the red buoy popped to the surface of the sea. The buoy would have been sent up by our scouts at the temple. The Seademons would not let us take any more stones away today. On the beach below us I saw Mihangel and Cularen's neat formations of silver, penguin-like creatures suddenly rise and straighten their ranks. Almost at the same moment the outline of each Hound blurred in a purplish-blue haze as they snapped on their force shields, which would give some protection against a suit puncture even if the extra power pack would make them heavier and slower. They moved like eggs of purplish-blue light into the water, sinking slowly like smooth, polished stones, two companies of them.

"Lady?" Captain Ian spoke to me over the radio. "We should be getting ready."

"Tell the company, then," I radioed back.

The sergeants and corporals began getting their squads into their helmets and ushering them onto the aircars, whose rotors had been turned on, so that the whine rose steady and fast. I had climbed into the lead aircar and had slipped my fins over my boots when Caven tapped my shoulder. I turned to see a dead Seademon floating on the surface like a red feather with a fat, heavy quill. Another body rose to the surface. Dimly through my helmet I could hear the others cheering. A yellow marker buoy suddenly popped to the surface with a splash. Mihangel and Cularen had reached the temple with their companies.

I could hear other commanders shouting to their companies over the radio now, their voices mixing with the disorganized cries and grunts rising disembodied from beneath the bay. It looked so peaceful right now, even with the litter of bodies on the surface. And every now and then I'd hear a human cry and it would be like a knife inside me as I wondered who it was. And once a wounded Seademon jetted to the surface, skimming along for a few seconds before it seemed to collapse in the water. After that, it glided under its own momentum until a current caught it, sweeping it out toward the sea.

Suddenly the pilot in front of us revved his motors higher and the dust began to rise in the man-made wind there on the cliff. Our aircar seemed to leap from the cliff, or rather the cliffside seemed to drop away violently. We soared over the sea, zooming on past the temple.

Caven crouched behind the pilot, scanning the horizon intently. Beneath us I saw a large purplish-red cloud staining the sea water. It must have been a swarm of Seademons rising to defend their sanctuary. Then we passed beyond the Seademons to a large patch of sea that was a deeper red than the rest because of the trench that began here in the continental slope. The trench was Caven's landmark.

"About here," I heard him radio to the pilot. And the pilot released a jet of strong yellow dye. He banked sharply after two hundred meters and then again after another two hundred meters until he had formed a U shape on the surface of the water. The rest of the flotilla moved over the drop zone, and our pilot resumed his old position.

I heard Da's voice so calm and unconcerned telling us to go now. The pilot dropped the aircar sharply out of the sky, cutting in his rotors again only when we were a few feet from the surface. Water rose up in sheets, spraying all of us so that it felt as if we were in a rainstorm. "Snap on your force shields," I radioed to my company. I heard other company commanders giving the same order to their units in the flotilla. I was looking at Caven when he snapped his on. I couldn't see his face behind his visor any more in the haze about him. I did the same and the world became a little hazier. "Let's go, Captain." The Hounds in our aircar got into position on both sides of the car, which rocked under the sudden shift in balance. The Hounds swung their shimmering legs over the sides. "Jump." They landed with huge splashes in the water. All around us in the aircar, the others were jumping too.

Caven gripped my shoulder and his helmet touched mine. "Go back, Ciaran. Go back before it's too late."

"Who'll guard your back?" I said. Together we clambered over the side. On the red-brown surface of the sea were circles of foam where the others had already gone in. My feet hit the surface with a crash and a shock that made my knees buckle and I went into the water flailing. And I had practiced the jump over and over just to prevent such an entrance. For a moment I couldn't see because of all the air bubbles—as if I were hidden in chains of silver beads, but the chains thinned out and the beads became smaller and I could see other suited Hounds moving slowly in the gloom, waving their arms and kicking their legs as they began to form up.

I couldn't find Caven or Ardui. I looked for other Hounds in my company, but I didn't see any suits that looked familiar. Much to my chagrin, I realized that I'd lost my company somehow; perhaps I hadn't come out of my dive soon enough. Well, I wouldn't be the first person to lose his or her command; Da himself had plenty of stories about such things. The only thing to do was hook up with the nearest group.

They were slipping their crossbows off their shoulder clips. I did the same, notching back the nylar string and slipping in a magazine of rapid-fire darts with the little explosive gel heads. Overhead, the surface of the water gleamed a golden red as if someone had set fire to the sea, and the light went shimmering and writhing snake-like about us in long, thin ribbons.

Ahead of us, ghost-like in the dimness, I saw the small undersea mountain rising out of the darkness, as if the black night itself were taking tangible shape. And on the peak of the mountain were huge slabs of stone, easily ten meters long and five meters wide.

Between us and the temple rose the Seademons. At this distance, they glittered like a red cloud of tiny flashing specks, streaming now in one direction and then darting in another—as if the cloud pulsed and changed shape. I knew the cloud was really the army of the Seademons. The red cloud seemed to extend endlessly into the dark.

The other Hounds began moving downward and I knew I'd been right when I thought they weren't my company because my company was supposed to have moved forward at a depth of ten meters. I looked up and saw several groups, like schools of bloated minnows, swimming toward the temple. I couldn't figure out which one was my company because while I had been getting my bearings I might have wandered horizontally as well as vertically. Other groups were moving downward too, so I hurried to follow the company I'd joined.

It was as if I were part of an old silver-mesh theater curtain unrolling slowly downward in the twilight as more and more groups fell out to hover at their assigned depth. But my new company didn't stop until we were at sixty meters, at the very edge of visible light where colours became mere memories and everything appeared as shades of grey and white, their shapes blurred and indistinct. The blackness of the abyss yawned beneath us and I felt that if I ever started falling into that, I would never return.

I looked back at the surface of the sea, now so far away. At this distance it seemed to be a sheet of pure golden white —as if I'd found the outer wall of the Universe beyond which lay the Prime Mover, the Ideal; and the Hounds all

161

about and above me were simply shadows created by that fire. And even as I watched, the other groups overhead began moving forward. The bottom companies were to move last so that we could guard against any surprise attack from below. Behind and above us were the four companies of the reserve battalion, headed by Colonel Donogh, an old friend of Da's, and as canny a warhound as ever lived.

I chinned on the infrared scanner. It was as if I were seeing the Hounds for what they truly were: dark, shadowy flesh changed to a source of never-ending light. The Hound next to me moved and because the particles of my visor were slow to change—"remembering" the last position of the figure—the Hound's arms and legs seemed to have grown long gossamer wings.

Then over the radio I heard the commander, a woman with a shrill voice. She was Captain Donall, who had been Athvel's adjutant. With Athvel's disappearance, she had been given the company, though its members still referred to themselves as Athvel's Own. I had heard that they had asked for—*claimed* might be a better word—the most dangerous position of all. On Captain Donall's order, the company gave a kick, surging forward in an irresistible tide with the other companies.

The closer we drew to the cloud of Seademons, the more the cloud seemed to disintegrate into thick, angry, white motes; and the closer we swam, the more the motes became like long, tapering, cone-shaped, white-hot coals with fine tendrils of smoke—or a field of restless, long-petaled flowers.

I looked down at the depths and saw more white dots rising fast. I checked my knife; it was ready in its sheath on my left sleeve. On command we fell back about thirty meters, crossbows cocked and ready. We seemed so slow and clumsy compared to the Seademons in front of us, who jetted after us like comets flying from the sun, tails stream-

162

ing before them. The Seademons below tried to change direction toward our new position, but instead rammed into the ones in front of us. We halted as the Seademons milled about in momentary confusion.

I fired with everyone else when ordered. I shot ahead of me, moving my crossbow in a slow circle, as we'd all been trained to do, covering a certain area ahead of me. If everyone else did the same, a pattern of darts would be laid down that would be impossible to escape. I could feel the crossbow jerking in my hands as the hook slid back and forth in the channel, pulling the nylar string back taut, releasing it with a quick jerk, and then hooking it back again automatically. All this in only a second, like some smooth-pounding piston. I was continually having to slip the old clip out and put in a new one.

And the blackness of the sea was filled with angry grey puffs, like little balls of wool that appeared suddenly in the dark—like strange night flowers suddenly blossoming among the Seademons. A shrill, high keening began. And the cloud of Seademons stirred in even greater confusion as corpses rose upward or wounded Seademons jetted back and forth, ramming their friends and changing direction only to ram others.

The volley started getting a little ragged, explosions occurring after I and the others were already reloading our crossbows; and I remember being angry at those other Hounds who were firing too slow, but it could easily have been myself who was firing too fast along with the others around me.

It was as if someone had harvested the Seademons, for the cloud seemed thinner against the blackness. The Seademons who were left milled about uncertainly, darting this way and that in short, quick, unsure jerks. We fired again and the volleys became even longer and more ragged than before. The Seademons began to charge then, not in any concerted action, but in ones and twos, as if there were no leaders left but only reckless individuals bent upon some kind of revenge.

I heard Captain Donall tell us to fire at will. I got my clip in as soon as I could and began to fire at anything ahead of me, watching the visor of my helmet as intently as a gunner tracks a target on the radarscope. Suddenly a Seademon was among us, glowing an eerie white. Its tentacles rose and fell faster than the screen could follow, so it seemed to have a hundred tentacles. Its coral sword bashed its way through the force screen of one suit, cutting the suit open so that the air exploded outward in a rush of silver bubbles. I heard the scream, muffled by the man's helmet. His suit would seal over the cut, but the man was already dead, his body floating; beginning to cool off, it changed from white to soft, dull grey.

And then the Seademon had another Hound in its tentacles. It was almost as if she were wrapped in coils and spirals of white light. And there wasn't anything to do but move in. I let go of my crossbow so that it dangled from the strap hooked to my belt, and I drew out my sheath knife. Other Hounds swam at the same time into that giant, anemone-like Seademon, its tentacles flailing wildly about. I could see a blur of white in front of me and cut at what my helmet showed as blackness but what I was sure would be a tentacle—there was a slight delay in registering information on the screen. And the fine steel of the knife thudded into something and sliced through it even as the tentacle finally appeared on the screen with my knife just about to cut it. I could hear the screams from the Seademon as the other Hounds hacked away at it. The water about us became like a glowing cloud from the hot ichor flowing from the demon.

One of the other Hounds was dragging the wounded Hound away. She kept her arms out stiff, though she managed to kick her legs. I suppose she might have broken some ribs if not an arm or two. Someone tapped the button on her breather pack and her suit began to swell until she looked like a large balloon. She was passed back to the medics. I was still a little shaky from the fight when I heard Captain Donall again. I resheathed my knife and retrieved my crossbow from where it dangled from my waist, beginning then to kick my way upward. Behind us I knew the reserve was moving down to cover us. It was time to close the trap, for we would form the bottom of a cage while the Hounds above us would form its walls, surrounding the Seademons. Even though the Seademons outnumbered us, our superior weapons let us swim in much looser formation than they could. It took fewer Hounds to cover the same area than it did Seademons.

We stopped about thirty meters from the surface. Above us was an angrily swirling nebula of humans and whip-like forms wrestling with one another, as if in some eternal struggle. We drove the Seademons we had fought into the muddle above us. From far above me I heard the commanders of the Hounds ordering a withdrawal. Slowly the humans fought free and withdrew till they formed a circle some two hundred meters in diameter. We were to use special clips now that would self-explode after traveling some hundred and fifty meters—another of Mihangel's inventions. That way if a Hound fired at a Seademon, he or she wasn't likely to hit the person opposite.

The Seademons finally settled into a huge global formation, revolving in the water. It no longer seemed like a battle but like teasing some wild, white-celled creature that threw itself first this way and that against the sides of a jar, and as it crashed about, the white-celled globe shrank more and more. We would have let the Seademons surrender. We wanted to communicate with them, after all, and more than once we stopped firing to give them an opportunity to call a truce, but that only seemed to make them wilder and their charges grew more impulsive. They would not stop until they were all dead.

After it was over, I swam up slowly toward the surface, switching off my infrared scanner when I thought I was near it. But it was still dark overhead—not because the sun was setting but because the Seademons covered the surface. The sea for miles around was clogged with their corpses, and the birds lined the cliffsides as they rested from feasting and even more rode the bobbing corpses and gorged themselves. The voices of the birds made a steady wall of noise that echoed and re-echoed against the rocks. Here and there patches of Seademons would be lost under the fluttering, squawking flocks of feeding birds.

I had to shove my way up between two dead Seademons, sending a cloud of birds protesting into the air. The bodies all about me were twitching because there were other Hounds trying to push their way up. I would be fighting my way through corpses if I tried to swim on the surface. Instead I dove back down and kicked my way under the bodies toward the stormy slope ahead where the surf action tossed the sand about in a blurred cloud.

I went to Da's headquarters on the highest point of the cliffs, knowing that Caven would look for me there eventually. I was covered with the ichor from the Seademons, but I was too tired to wash the sticky stuff off. Insects immediately began buzzing about me to lick at the ichor on my suit. I took my helmet off anyway and almost gagged at the charnel smell.

Phoil saw me and tapped Da, waving in my direction. Da turned. He was wearing a command helmet, more squat and bulbous than a regular one, with small antennae rising from either side so that he looked like some horned war god—or giant carrion insect. As was his usual custom, he had his sword with him, a kind of claymore. Though the blade was heavy enough, he handled his sword easily, using it like a pointer. He pointed his sword at me now and shouted to make himself heard through his helmet: "What are you doing here?"

"The same as you," I said doggedly.

"You're my heir now. What if something had happened to you?" Suddenly he broke into a grin. "Couldn't stay away when you smelled a good fight brewing. Well, I can't blame you for that. It's in our blood." He waved his sword at my helmet. "Best put that back on."

"Later." I moved away from him to sit down on a rock where the winds blew some of the smell of death away from me. My crossbow still dangled from my waist. Tiredly I unclipped it and rehooked it to the shoulder clip where it usually hung. At the last moment I remembered to put it on safety.

Suddenly my scalp lock, which I had worn in a clubbed knot at the back of my head, felt too tight. I pulled the pins away so it spilled down free, not caring if it mixed with the ichor on my suit. A very tired-looking Mihangel and Cularen stopped by on their way to report to Da.

"Your hair will stick to your suit." With his gloved hand, Mihangel tried to place my scalp lock on a less sticky part of my suit, but there was none.

"You've a strange way of taking care of our holding," Cularen added. He had his helmet under his arm, as did Mihangel. "I thought you were supposed to stay there and watch things."

"I wish I had."

"Leave her be," Mihangel advised Cularen. "We should be seeing Da."

I sat for a long time, paying attention to nothing, so I only heard the last part of their conversation.

"We've broken their proud might," Da was saying. He

167

swung his sword to include the entire sea. "They'll no more be troubling our shores."

"And Athvel and his son?" Mihangel asked gloomily. "What of them?"

Da touched Mihangel's arm. "Your children will grow up free and safe because of this day and you'll bless the sacrifice of your brother and nephew." Da seemed to be saying that more for himself than for Mihangel and Cularen. I noticed suddenly how all the troubles of the last few years had whitened Da's hair. In fact, he looked rather old.

"The Lady's here, Caven," I heard Ardui say.

"Thank the One," murmured Eriu, who was at Caven's side.

Caven leaned over me. In his hand he held a canteen of water from some stream he had found. He'd also managed to wash the ichor off his suit. "Fetch more water for the Lady," Caven ordered Ardui, and Ardui ran back down the path obediently.

"Your hair's getting dirty." In distress, Eriu held my scalp lock against the back of my head while I took the canteen from Caven. I tried to hold it to my mouth, but my hands were shaking.

"Here," he said gently and held it for me, tipping it up so that the water poured gently into my mouth. His eyes were pained by what we had seen and done there that day. And from somewhere far out to sea it seemed to me that I could hear a moan—as if some giant thing were beginning to stir in its sleep.

nine

I

We did not see one Seademon for an entire year, let alone speak to any. And there was no opportunity to discover the fate of Athvel or of Iriel, his son. They were lost to us, but —or so we told ourselves—we'd gained the mastery of our world at last. The rectors doubted that there had ever been many Seademons and assumed that the bulk of their male population had died trying to defend their temple: all the dead had been males, as we learned when the rectors had dissected several corpses. We swept the seas periodically, but found nothing. And not one came even when we destroyed the rest of their temple. All that we left in the sea were the thousands of whitening Seademon skeletons—the continental slope was carpeted with their bones.

The Tearless One had said nothing upon our return. She sat all day in her room, hardly noticing when day passed into night. She ate whatever was given her, but her hands and mouth moved mechanically, so I was surprised when I received her note, written in the large, childish scrawl she had learned from the Anglic. Caven was afraid at first; but when he saw that I was set on going, he gave in. After all, this was the first attempt by the Tearless One to communicate with anyone; and though I had my reasons to hate her, yet in my heart I had forgiven her. After all, she had never asked to be brought here or raised by our ways.

Her frowning, sullen guard admitted me to her room. The light came through the panes of glass softly and I saw the Tearless One sitting on a pallet. I stopped beside her, waiting for her to notice me. The year's silent isolation had changed her. It was hard to think of her being only twenty in true years. Though her face was youthful, yet she now gave the impression that there were depths to her soul beyond the measuring of time and that within those depths flowed timeless powers that ran like the great currents beneath the calm surface of the sea.

She tugged at my hands suddenly. It felt as slight and yet as irresistible as the tugging of the surf when you try to stand in the water at high tide.

"Ciaran must go away. Take her man and her child and go far away. Into the hills away from the sea."

"Will the . . ." I tried to remember what she had called the Seademons. "Will the Bringers try to attack us?"

"No, there are too few Bringers left."

"Then this is probably the safest place for us. After all, every man and woman is a warrior here, and there are mine fields ringing the mouth of the bay."

She gave my hands a little squeeze as if she could press her message into my flesh. "Ciaran does not yet know of all the powers and forces of this world. For Ciaran's own sake, be away from this place before tonight."

I stared down into the Tearless One's eyes. "What will happen? Who has told you all this?"

The Tearless One let go of my hands. She shrank from me. "Maeve has talked to none of the sea folk. None. But Maeve can listen to the sea through the walls, and the sea has changed. She will rise tonight."

"Do you mean the sea? Is *she* the sea?"

But she seemed to withdraw, like the tide pulling away from the land: it was beyond any person's stopping. It was as if she were afraid that she had already said too much. I tried to speak to her and draw her back, but she would only look at a spot on the wall.

When I reached our house, I started to get out our journey bags and told Eriu to prepare for an overnight trip. Though Eriu was now a full-fledged Hound, she had asked to stay on as my maid.

Caven put his fist on his hip. "What are you doing?"

"The Tearless One warned us to be away tonight. I'm going to humor her. It won't do any harm."

"Folk will laugh at us."

"I'm not so small as to be unable to hear some laughter at my expense, not if it means helping some poor creature back to sanity."

Losgann, nearly three, fell and began to cry. Caven picked up Losgann and dangled him on his hip for a bit. "And supposing she's right?" he asked thoughtfully.

Later on, I tried to talk to Da, but he scoffed at everything I said.

"If you want to act like a witched woman," he said to me, "that is your prerogative. But we have little to fear on either land or sea now."

But when I returned home, I found the Worldlies had gathered—all the little ones I had helped at the rectory and some of the others born and raised at other holdings but come here for training. There were also a few of the younger Shippies who remembered little of the Long Flight and who knew and respected a fellow Shippy like Caven. There were even a dozen or so Hounds from my company.

Caven sat outside our house in the middle of our piled belongings, Losgann already strapped in his traveling rig to Caven's back. Eriu spread her arms helplessly. "All these people came when they heard that the Tearless One wanted to speak with you."

Embarrassed, I got up on the bench before our house. "I humor the Tearless One is all," I announced to them. "She has had this strange fancy and will become upset if I do not seem to believe her."

"And yet—" Ardui shouldered his way forward through the crowd—"she knows this world as no other creature who can speak to us. What did she say?"

"That we must be away from here before nightfall, up into the hills. There is some danger from the sea."

They all looked rather thoughtful for a moment. People bent their heads to talk with their neighbors, and my cheeks grew steadily redder as the murmuring grew. Finally, one of the older Hounds—I recognized him as a sergeant major in my company—stepped up to the picket fence. "We have little reason to love her, and yet she knows much. Lady, will you take us with you and show us this safe spot?"

So I led some fifty families and their stumpies through the ripe fields of wheat into the northeastern hills until we reached the old doom of the Anglic. Dust and branches and chitters had taken up occupancy inside, but we cleaned all of them out along with the debris of the destruction of the doom. We hung hides over the now paneless frames and installed the children inside. We adults camped around the doom and it began to seem like a picnic.

When night fell, I moved away from the others a little so I could look down on the shining lamps of the holding below. Farther on, the waters of the bay danced under the moonlight like some thick black veil sewn with silver thread. I sat on a rock, the air thick with the smells of fall. I heard heavy boots crush a path through the thick weeds that now grew about the Anglic's doom.

"What's in your mind, Ciaran?" Caven asked.

"I'll feel like such a fool tomorrow when nothing has happened."

"At least you have the Tearless One talking to you again. That's—" He stopped. The waters of the bay had begun stirring, like a veil drifting about in the breeze . . . shifting gently . . . moving slowly, about to reveal the true face of some dark, terrible god.

Klaxons began hooting below. I suppose the sonar had picked up something. "We should be down there with the musterings," I said. "I didn't think—"

Aircars shot screaming into the sky, their lights gleaming like clusters of stars. The water seemed to drain from the bay for a moment, and Caven frowned. "It's not low tide yet." And then the water rolled in again like a huge black-lacquered sheet. For a moment I thought it would crack against the shore and not surge and crash like water.

Mines had been placed across the mouth of the bay, both on the surface and at different depths below, in case there were simultaneous attacks being launched. We saw them explode, the ones on the surface bursting like stars, the ones below like puffs of light seen through a dark mist.

And suddenly it was as if a grove of giant trees, each a half-kilometer high, sprang from the surface of the sea. They wavered for a moment as if shaken by some invisible wind, and the tips of the red columns hollowed and then expanded; we could hear the rasp and hiss even from this distance. And then the giant tentacles dipped sinuously down to grope about within the holding until they gave the creature some purchase.

The sea heaved and swelled. We saw the breakers crash down above the breakwater at the very beginning of the cottages of the holding. The giant eyes, one on either side of the body, half rose from the water. The rest of the body filled the bay.

"It's like a gigantic Seademon," Caven said in an awed voice.

"Remember those rock carvings that you and Athvel found that first time you went south?" I could feel a curious tingling sensation at the base of my spine. "Those carvings were actually in perspective. She's the Bearer. She's one of the females. The Tearless One tried to tell me, but I couldn't understand her."

Along the tentacles I could see black smudges: the mines must have seemed like pinpricks to her.

The aircars swarmed near her eyes, darting in and out of the weaving forest of tentacles. And sometimes two tentacles would catch an aircar between them, closing with a crunching finality, but the other aircars bounced and slid and rolled over the coiling tentacles that tried to catch them. And suddenly all the arms came down into the bay and a huge pillar of water fountained up. The aircars were caught before they could dart away and they were swept into the bay, where they sank, leaving white spots dotting the surface of the bay. In the ominous silence that followed, we could hear the soft popping of power rifles or the chatter of automatic weapons. Since we had never expected an enemy to get in this close to the heart of the colony, our missile and gun batteries had not been placed to fire directly at the holding. The sounds of small-arms fire seemed futile as they tried to fill up the vast emptiness of the night. Gunfire licked at the monster from all over the holding, but it might have been like spiders throwing their strands over some human for all that she noticed.

She rose higher so that the great eyes, large now as two terrible and yet beautiful moons, seemed to hover above the bay for a moment. A missile screamed across the night sky and fell somewhere out to sea, throwing up a geyser of water with the explosion. The batteries could not get the proper angle. The Bearer angrily brought her tentacles down with a wind-roaring sound as if chunks of sky were falling. They crashed down within the holding, plowing through metal and glass and flesh and bone as if these were nothing, and gouging out large tracks in the dirt and sand.

The tentacles hollowed out as the mouths fastened themselves to the land and she pulled herself forward with a lurch. Outside the bay, little islands of her hide suddenly

174

appeared and the water flooded through the holding, surging into the fields. For a moment, the Bearer slid back into the bay and then forward again, throwing up a huge sheet of water before her that hid the dooms of the holding. The water raced across the fields to lap at the very foot of the hills where we stood. I doubted if any of the Folk in the holding had had a chance to put their diving suits on. We could hear the screams and groans and wails even from up here.

Then, her tentacles still firmly gripping the land, she pulled more and more of her body up into the bay. Her eyes rose higher and the sea surged halfway up the hills. There seemed to be no end to her height, her body seeming to cover a large part of the horizon. With loud popping noises her tentacles broke free from the shore and swung up and then down. They landed with an earth-shaking jar. Throughout the now darkened holding, glass panes shattered and steel frames screamed as they collapsed. The huge arms pounded and pounded at the land in a thunderous drumming roll. When she finally held her arms up, all sounds within the holding had stopped. There was only the sporadic roar of a missile being launched at her in a futile gesture since she was still at the wrong angle to be hit.

She shoved herself back into the sea, pushing hectare after hectare of glistening hide underneath the water. Her eyes gleamed beneath the surface like two distant fires, blurred and distorted, and the sea rushed back into the bay, foaming and hissing about the tips of her arms, which were the only things to remain above the bay. The headland at the mouth of the bay crumbled—I suppose she had brushed it as she withdrew. And then the terrible eyes were gone, as if we had seen them only in a dream.

The gun and missile batteries fired in wide, sweeping patterns; but they had not been designed to hit targets beneath the water. While the missiles and shells roared overhead, we started searching among the hills and found

175

some survivors clinging to an aircar. They told us how Da had stood alone there in the ruins of Doom Devlin. The sea had ebbed momentarily and the foam was bubbling everywhere, hissing and disappearing into the sand that now half covered everything.

Da had stood alone, a white-haired old man, and he had raised his sword, the only weapon he had left. "To me, Hounds of Ard-Ri, to me!" He had swung the sword over his head so that it shone in the moonlight. And there was a kind of grandeur about him standing there, facing the sea and the creature.

Prime Rector Phoil had shouted to Da to come to the aircar. And Phoil had gotten down from the car to pull Da back, for of that group only Phoil would dare lay hands upon Da. But Da shook Phoil off. And then the others had shouted to the Prime Rector to save himself.

But Phoil was caught up in the madness that has always been the curse of the Folk and had slipped out his dagger and taken his place beside Da.

And what shall I say? What can I say about the bravery and nobility and foolishness? Mihangel and Cularen threw off their jackets and the one picked up a hoe and the other a rake and they marched back to range themselves on either side of Phoil and their old Lord. The people still in the aircar or clinging to its sides looked toward Da and his stepsons and the Prime Rector, a last ragged line: frail humans pitting themselves against the might of the sea.

The foolishness of it! The magnificent foolishness. They answered that challenge in the only way they understood—with one last battle. The creature loomed higher and higher. The moonlight shimmered on her head and beneath that head, on a green-black crystal wall fifteen meters high.

And Da had waved his sword and shouted and the others had all shouted with him. But the roar of the wave drowned out the end of their battle cry. And the Folk saw them silhouetted for a moment there on the shoreline; and then the ruins and the Lord and his stepsons and the Prime Rector disappeared in the wave. As if they had been apotheosized, taken up, subsumed from this material world finally into their legend—as was fitting.

And the wave had swept on, catching up the aircar. Men and women and children were tossed out of the wreck, and others were torn away as they tried to grip its sides. The aircar had gone spinning, spinning, spinning on top of the wave, tossed along to the very hills, where it lodged in a tree. It was there we found them.

II

The next morning I went down from the hill to walk among the ruins, and the others followed but at a polite distance. Drowned bodies lay among the broken crystal panes; and the steel beams of the dooms looked as if they had been twisted by giant hands. The slate houses had all collapsed, their walls and roofs cracked into hundreds of pieces. The rectory was totally destroyed, the relics and the library of books and microfilms all lost or ruined by the sea water. All that was left of our ancient knowledge was what I had taken up with me into the hills or what might lie in the other holdings. Though only one third of the population lived at Da's holding, it had been the mind and heart of the colony.

Here and there I could hear a child crying, but for the most part we were silent as we walked on to the very edge of the sea. The mud squelched beneath my boots as I looked about. Eriu, carrying Losgann, followed me at a distance. She seemed afraid to lose sight of me and yet afraid to disturb my thoughts. Only Caven dared to join me. He frowned and shook his head. "It's no good. I can't find their bodies anywhere."

"They were probably washed out to sea."

"So much was lost," Caven sighed. "The aircars. The central computer."

"No sense counting what we lost," I said. "Better to count what we still have."

"Lady . . ." The sergeant major from my old company shambled along. "Lady, the children are hungry."

"What?"

"The children are hungry, Lady. What shall we do?"

I stopped for a moment, aware of all eyes upon me. I was almost the last of the Devlins. It made me feel wild and sad and angry inside . . . and lost.

I thought of their faces: Da and Athvel and Mihangel and Cularen, all of them claimed by that peacock's tail of a sea, as if the peacock sea had stretched its tail over them and brushed them away into nothingness. Though I was only twenty-four, I felt more like eighty-four.

"Have men . . . Have men go out and bring back wood for fires." Once I got started, it began to be easier. "And have other men go into the fallout shelters. They'll find emergency supplies there."

"That's for when the Fair Folk come," Caven said.

"The Fair Folk. The Fair Folk. All my life we've watched the stars and never had time to see the mud and sea about us. We'll take one thing at a time. Right now we'll use some of those supplies until you can organize hunting parties tomorrow and see what things you can find in storage at the other holdings."

Caven bowed his head silently. I noticed how all the others were standing up just a little straighter now. I pointed to Ardui. "Ardui, see to digging latrines and finding an unpolluted source of water. I won't have plague running through us too."

I began giving instructions to others then. After all, we had to go on living. Caven brought me a cup of whiskey and we sipped together from the same battered tin cup. "The

178

Curse." Caven looked sad. "It's come full force."

"The fulfilling of the Lady's Curse was of our own making. If we had lived *with* this world instead of against it, the Lady Daedre would have been wrong."

"Surely there's nothing more that could be asked of us."

But right then a boy came running up. In his hands he gripped a crossbow—the mechanism, though, had been so knocked about that it couldn't have been fired. "Lady, they're coming."

"By the One!" Caven said. The bay was bubbling again like a giant cauldron come aboil. And we could see the red-gleaming, jeweled backs rising out of the water, a hundred Seademons, and all of them with their coral swords and bone war clubs. They must have been in enormous pain from the light, but somehow they stood it all. Balanced on the back of the largest was the Tearless One, looking as if she were sliding along the surface of the sea rather than riding. And in her arms was a child.

The Tearless One stepped down nimbly from the back of the great one-eyed Seademon onto the beach. She waited at the spot where the surf, rushing to its highest line, would foam about her ankles.

Caven raised his crossbow.

I pushed it down. "No."

The others murmured and stirred, and Caven looked at me angrily. "Are you forgetting how she destroyed your family?"

"Maeve wasn't responsible. They destroyed themselves." I began to walk down to the surf line.

There were frightened cries from the Folk, and Ardui started down to intercept me. "Lady, let one of us go to hear her demands. You are almost the last of your line."

"And so it's fitting that I be the one to parley." I waved him back and reluctantly he obeyed.

The Tearless One and I stared at one another for a time.

"Everything is balanced," the Tearless One finally an-

179

nounced, "and the Sea Folk would have peace with Ciaran's Folk. And as pledge of peace, Maeve and Ciaran will exchange children."

I hesitated. This was more than some wild idea of the Tearless One, I felt, for she held Iriel carefully in her arms and seemed as reluctant as any human parent to give up her child.

She leaned forward, speaking in an urgent tone. "The Sea Folk do not understand parenthood. The eggs are laid in broods and tended not by the father or his kin but by his sword brothers. The whole concept of single birth and the selfish owning of one child is monstrous to them."

I suppose we were being tested somehow by the Seademons. "Is this to bring peace and understanding?"

"It is hard for Maeve too," she explained, "but the Bringers will raise Ciaran's son as they would one of their own. And Ciaran will raise Iriel as her son. When they are both of age, Ciaran's son will be returned to her and Iriel will go among the Bringers so that there may be a person among each of the two peoples who can understand and explain the ways of the other." She studied my face when I remained silent. "Ciaran does not trust Maeve."

"Should I?"

It began at the corners of her eyes, small glints of reflected light that slowly became little beads of moisture, the beads growing larger and larger until they welled outward of their own weight to streak down her cheeks. She leaned forward so that, while she held on to Iriel, she could brush her cheeks with the back of her hand. For a moment she stared uncomprehendingly at the moisture there.

"You're crying tears," I said in wonder.

"It . . . It is so strange," said Maeve—she was the Tearless One no longer.

"Why are you crying?"

"Maeve does not know." She shook her head in bewilderment. "It just happened. This aching began deep inside her and rose to her eyes."

"And what was the ache for?"

"Because the killing should end here, today, but it will not."

"Perhaps it will."

Crossbow in hand, Caven stormed down to the beach. The Seademons roused.

"Throw your crossbow away," I hissed to him. He had enough presence of mind to do what I said.

"It's monstrous," he said to her, "to think we'd give up our child."

"To the Seademons *we* are the ones who are the monsters," I reminded him. Caven looked at me in confusion. I think for the first time he fully realized that I must now be more than his friend and wife and mother to our children. I was the last of the Devlins and must now act for the safety of the Folk.

"But Losgann—how can you think of giving him up?" His voice shook. "If you summon the Folk, they'll answer you, Ciaran. They'll come from the shepherd's hut and the farmer's holding, just to fight for you."

"If we keep to our old ways, we'll raise Losgann to meet the same fate as the rest of my family."

Caven looked away, deeply hurt inside and unreachable, as if he had withdrawn into some inner fortress. And I felt as if some part of me had been cut away. I touched his arm. "Caven, please try to forgive me."

"Aye, well . . ." He shrugged and seemed at least partly reconciled to the matter. "Do what you must, then." He was loyal to the Devlins even if he did not understand what I was doing. And an exchange of hostages, though hard, was nothing new.

The Tearless One smiled then and raised her hand.

"And as Ciaran's Folk are now without food, we give this to you."

A silver cloud shimmered suddenly beneath the surface of the water, flowing quickly toward the beach. I tensed, expecting some new monster, but the silver cloud broke the surface and fat tuna-like fish, each easily fifty kilos, skimmed through the water, frightened by the hooting Seademons which goaded them along with whip-like cracks of their tentacles. And they did not stop even when they came to the beach, but leaped out of the surf onto the sand. It was like a living spray of flesh pouring itself onto the beach. I looked, stunned, at the huge pile of silver bodies that lay flapping and heaving and panting.

The Tearless One turned around, unable to hide her triumphant feelings. "Once this world belonged only to the Sea Folk, but they are willing to share it with Ciaran's Folk."

"That was never our way before, but it will be now," I said firmly. I glanced at Caven.

He hung his head and spoke heavily. "Well, I'll go fetch Losgann, then."

III

The people would not sleep by the beach or in the old ruins, preferring to sleep in the hills. By that time we had managed to establish contact with the holdings that had been untouched by the disaster. We'd gotten blankets and other things from some of the closer ones, with more things to come the next day from the farther holdings. But the state of the colony was to be sadly reduced now from what we once had known. If only we could keep from losing anything more.

It was twilight time, the time of the One, when so many revelations came to the learned rectors of the tales like the tale of Sane Collen, for this is the time when the world is suspended between thought and act. Caven crouched upon the hillside beside a small fire of his own making, working at a log of driftwood that he had found on the beach and insisted that some men help him carry back up here. His hammer made small tapping noises as his chisel slowly bit at the wood. Small, curling chips of wood lay piled about his feet up to his ankles. Outside of giving orders to the others to help him fetch the driftwood, he had said nothing since I had given Losgann to Maeve.

With Iriel in my own arms now, I walked over to him. He had worked deliberately and quickly at the log, carving two rough figures, one on either side of the log. They squatted with a certain strength; their eyes, though crudely outlined, possessed a definite force. Even only roughed out, the faces of both figures were the Devlin face: the face of Da, of Athvel, and of both Losganns.

"Will you not have some supper?" I asked.

Caven paused, wiping at his sweating forehead and leaving a chip clinging there. He set down his hammer and small chisel. "Aye," he said finally. "I'm finished for the night."

I called to one of the boys by the supper fire to fetch a plate over to Caven. I sat down beside him. He very studiously kept his eyes on the log rather than look at me. "What are you making?" I asked.

"I don't know. It was as if I heard the statue whispering to me from inside the log. I had to set it free." Caven held up his hands helplessly. "I've never felt anything like it." He took the plate from the boy with a nod of thanks. "Perhaps I'm possessed by the Anglic."

"When you're finished, we'll set it up by the beach, one face toward the land and one to the sea," I offered, "as a reminder to all of us."

Caven dipped his hands into the fish and porridge on his plate, selecting a piece of fish to stuff into his mouth. He was so tired and hungry he was beyond manners. He

183

chomped at it noisily while he considered my suggestion. Then he smiled dourly in his old way. "I wonder if the children will remember that it's only a statue." He leaned over to look at Iriel. "I wonder if this baby won't be sacrificing sheep to it."

I cradled Iriel in my arms. He lay so small and helpless. "And will he be wearing furs and swinging a stone ax?"

Caven set his plate down, sticking his fingers into his mouth to pull out some fish bones. The sky overhead was all dark except for one brilliant patch of purple on the horizon. Finally, he shrugged. "Maybe it won't be such a bad thing if he does."

Caven took a branch and threw it onto the fire beside us. The sap oozed from the wood, hissing and popping so that he had to move back a little from the sparks. It brought him closer to me. "Deep thoughts are more in *your* line, Ciaran." He hunched forward, his chin propped on his knees. "But the true time of the One is the twilight, when things are neither all of shadow nor of light. It's the nature of the One to change and always to be changing and taking new form. But we've always been a people who have stood against change all these true centuries." He twisted his head in my direction to see if I was laughing at him.

But I wasn't. I only nodded. "Aye, maybe to be human is not to stay the same as you were a thousand, two thousand years ago. It's to change and to keep on changing to whatever the situation may require. And—" I stopped when Caven held a finger to his lips.

"I think the lad's asleep," he whispered. He leaned forward to study the child for a moment. "He does have Athvel's look, all right."

I rocked the child lightly. "So some of the older folk say." I added, "I've also heard some grumbling that I've brought a changeling among the Folk."

"That wee thing?" Caven scoffed. "What do they know? He's the heir, the true heir of this world as we could never

184

be. He and Losgann. Fancyfree will be their world as Tara was never ours."

I stifled a little yawn. "I think I'm a bit out of my depth if I'm to be seeing two thousand years ahead. Shall we just worry about getting through tomorrow?"

Caven gripped my shoulder lightly, almost shyly; and yet his strength and warmth seemed to flow into me. "We will. Somehow."